~ Retta Barre's Oregon Trail ~

BOOK ONE

THE LOST
WAGON TRAIN

⚜ STEPHEN BLY ⚜

CROSSWAY BOOKS

A DIVISION OF
GOOD NEWS PUBLISHERS
WHEATON, ILLINOIS

The Lost Wagon Train

Copyright © 2002 by Stephen Bly

Published by Crossway Books
           a division of Good News Publishers
           1300 Crescent Street
           Wheaton, Illinois 60187

Cover design: David LaPlaca

Cover illustrator: Bill Dodge

First printing 2002

Printed in the United States of America

Library of Congress Cataloging-in-Publication Data
Bly, Stephen A., 1944 -
    The lost wagon train / Stephen Bly.
        p.   cm. — (Retta Barre's Oregon Trail ; Book 1)
    Summary: In 1852, Retta, a twelve-year-old girl constantly looking
for adventure on the Oregon Trail, gets lost in a storm and shares
shelter and friendship with a Shoshone family.
    ISBN 1-58134-391-4 (TPB : alk. paper)
    1. Oregon National Historic Trail—Juvenile fiction. [1. Oregon National
Historic Trail—Fiction. 2. Overland journeys to the Pacific—Fiction.
3. Frontier and pioneer life—West (U.S.)—Fiction. 4. Shoshone Indians—
Fiction. 5. Indians of North America—Fiction. 6. West (U.S.)—Fiction.]
I. Title. II. Series.
PZ7.B6275 Lo   2002
[Fic]—dc21   2001007097
                                                             CIP

| 15 | 14 | 13 | 12 | 11 | 10 | 09 | 08 | 07 | 06 | 05 | 04 | 03 | 02 |
| 15 | 14 | 13 | 12 | 11 | 10 | 9 | 8 | 7 | 6 | 5 | 4 | 3 | 2 |

For
Katherine Davis

. . . Without ceasing I mention you in my prayers,
asking that somehow by God's will
I may now at last succeed in coming to you.

ROMANS 1:9-10 ESV

One

They waved flags on Main Street of Oregon City.

Children shouted.

Women waved.

Men cheered.

Boys whistled.

Retta Barre straddled the chestnut and white pinto and waved to the crowd. *People in Oregon are so friendly! I'm not sure if it's me or my horse that they like.*

She stopped the horse in the middle of the dirt street. "Now, boy, show them what you can do. Bow down on one knee. . . . I'll wave. . . . They love it!"

Retta Barre was in Oregon.

We made it. Nothing can go wrong now.

At the sound of the gunshot, Retta sat straight up, and the quilt tumbled to her lap. It was pitch-dark, but she heard talking. She flopped back down on the pillow.

Her mother's voice was soft, almost pained. "Time to get up, girls."

She heard her older sister Lerryn sit up next to her.

Retta propped herself up on her elbow. "Why do they have to wake everyone up with a gunshot?"

"Why do they have to wake us up at 4:00 A.M.?" her sister grumbled.

"Girls, you should be used to that by now," Mrs. Barre said as she lit a lamp. "You have chores. Papa is already working."

Retta fumbled for her dress.

"Are you wearing that purple dress again?" Lerryn asked.

"It's not purple. It's pansy plum."

"Are you going to wear the bonnet?"

"Of course not."

"Do you know you're the only girl in the wagon train who doesn't wear a bonnet?"

Retta grinned. "Yep." She began to lace up her high-top black shoes. "Do you want to trade chores? You make the fire, and I'll milk the cows."

"I'm not touching that stuff," Lerryn huffed. With a tiny mirror propped against a crate, she began combing her long blonde hair.

Retta licked her fingers and mashed down her wild dark brown bangs. "Well, it *is* dried up." She crawled over the top of some crates toward the front of the covered wagon.

"Are you going outside looking like that?" Lerryn demanded.

"This is the way I always look. Besides, I don't have to primp because I'm your little sister who looks like a ten-year-old boy, remember?"

"That's not what I meant when I said that," Lerryn mumbled.

"What did you mean?"

"Never mind. Go on with your chores."

Retta had a small fire glowing when her father hiked into their camp. "Hi, Papa. Did you see any Indians? Was there a buffalo stampede? Did the prairie pirates try to raid camp? Did the horses run off with a wild stallion? Did a mountain lion sneak into the ox pen?"

Mr. Barre laughed and then licked his fingers and smoothed down the back of her hair.

"Oh, darlin', I'm afraid it was just another boring night on the trail."

"Well, at least my dreams are exciting!" she said.

"You aren't dreamin' of boys again, are you?"

"Papa! Lerryn is the one who dreams of boys . . . especially one boy. No, I was dreaming of the pinto for sale at Robidoux's. I dreamed I rode him all the way to Oregon."

"That's a good dream, darlin'. You reckon you could dream me up some coffee?"

"I was just about to do that."

"How's Mama? I think she had a rough night."

"I think she's okay," Retta replied. "But her voice sounded tired. Papa, do you think anything exciting is going to happen today?"

"You mean like an axle breaking or a mule running off or someone falling asleep and tumbling out of a wagon?"

"No, I'm thinking of a wagon sinking out of sight in quicksand, never to be seen again."

"Was there any particular wagon you wanted to sink in quicksand?"

"No, but I could probably think of one if I tried."

Mr. Barre grinned and ran his fingers through her tangled shoulder-length hair. "The MacGregor wagon is certainly the heaviest in the train. Now get that coffee boilin', and I'll go check on Mama."

By 7:00 A.M. the wagons creaked their way west parallel to the wide, shallow, treeless North Platte River. A dry, hot breeze rolled down from the northwest. For miles in every direction the short, tough buffalo grass painted every rolling hill and valley brown, broken only by gray sagebrush and an occasional spiked-leaf yucca or prickly pear cactus.

Retta's wagon was near the middle of the sixty-wagon train. She and her friends plodded along several hundred feet north of the wagons and out of the fog of dust that surrounded them.

"I ain't afraid of nothin'!" Ben insisted.

Retta locked her arms across her gingham dress. "Then pick it up."

"I don't want to," the boy replied, sticking out his dimpled chin.

Retta wrinkled her nose. "Ben Weaver, you're afraid to pick it up."

"I ain't neither." He kicked at the pale dirt with a worn brown boot. "I jist don't have time."

Retta glanced back at the endless line of covered wagons. "Oh? Where do you have to go, Ben?"

He tugged his suspenders over his shoulder and pointed to the hill in front of him. "To the river to look for a lost cow."

Retta raised her chin. "I don't see any lost cow."

"If you could see it, it wouldn't be lost. Besides, you girls are supposed to pick up them chips. Not us boys."

Retta stared down at the prairie dirt. "Why is it a girl's job?"

Ben shoved his thumbs in the front pockets of his brown ducking trousers. "It just is—that's all."

She glanced at the three girls behind her, each with a burlap sack over her shoulder. "I believe he's truly afraid to pick up a buffalo chip."

As Ben reached down, his blond hair curled out from under his floppy felt hat. He scooped up a bone-dry buffalo chip and sailed it right at Retta Barre. She ducked, and it landed at the other girls' feet.

"There. Are you happy?" he shouted and then trotted up the gradual rise of the brown grassy hill.

Retta Emily Barre wiggled her upturned nose, blew her bangs off her forehead, and grinned at the girls. "I told you I could talk him into picking one up."

Christen Weaver shifted the weight of the burlap sack to her other shoulder. "You told me you could sweet-talk my brother. I wouldn't exactly say that telling him he was afraid to touch buffalo dung was sweet talk."

"Especially since he threw it at you." Joslyn Jouppi's smile was bracketed by two fields of freckles.

"But he missed. And he did touch it. So there." Retta picked up the dried chip and dropped it into her sack.

Gilson bent her sloping shoulders and stepped up next to Retta. "How come picking up buffalo chips is a girl's job anyway?"

"Because, Gilson O'Day, no one else will do it—that's why," Joslyn blurted out.

"It's not so bad," Retta said. "We get to climb off those dusty covered wagons and visit with each other out here. I think I'd rather walk to Oregon City than ride on that wagon."

"But the sack is heavy," Gilson complained, her blonde hair swinging back from her pale face.

"I don't know how you do it without a bonnet," Christen said to Retta. "It's so hot."

"Retta's face is as brown as . . . as an Indian's," Joslyn declared. "I think. We haven't gotten close enough to see one yet."

"And that's just the way I like it." Christen shuddered. "I hear they like to kidnap girls and make them slaves."

"I wonder if they would make us pick up buffalo dung?" Joslyn murmured.

The yellow-brown soil was dry and silent under Retta's step. There was a fine taste of dust in her mouth. "Colonel Graves says that after Fort Bridger, we will wish we *had* buffalo chips."

Joslyn stroked her dark hair off her smooth white forehead and left a dirt streak. "I've been thinking maybe I won't go beyond Fort Hall."

Retta spun around. "Oh?"

Joslyn put her hand on her narrow, smooth chin. "Maybe I'll just find me a handsome soldier at Fort Hall and get married and settle down."

"Get married?" Christen gasped. "Joslyn, you are only twelve years old. You can't get married!"

"I'm very advanced for my age. Besides, at the rate we're going, I'll be thirty by the time we get to Fort Hall! We've been on the Oregon Trail for almost two months out of Independence, and we haven't seen the Rocky Mountains yet."

"Or an Indian battle," Christen added.

Gilson plopped her sack down on the dirt. "Or even a buffalo up close. They are always fifty miles away or something."

"Some things might be best seen from a distance." Retta shrugged.

"Just green grass, then brown grass and faded sky and a yellow sun," Joslyn said.

"And the stars at night," Retta added. "I think the stars are the most beautiful in the world out on the prairie."

"But they are the same old stars." Joslyn scooped up a dried chip and plopped it in her sack.

"But—but they are prettier," Retta insisted.

"My sack is getting heavy," Gilson murmured again as she changed it from one shoulder to the other. She coughed, and the girls paused until she caught her breath.

Retta shaded her eyes with her hand and looked across the prairie. "I wish I had my own pinto horse. William and Andrew have their own horses, but Mama says ladies don't ride horses. They only ride in carriages."

Christen stared at a buffalo chip at her feet. Retta picked it up and shoved it into Christen's sack.

"I think I'll ask Papa if I can buy myself a horse," Retta announced. "If I had had the money, I would have bought that pinto at Robidoux's."

Joslyn reached under the collar of her faded blue gingham dress and scratched her shoulder. "And just how are you going to buy a horse?"

Retta gazed across the distant grassy prairie and watched the heat rise off the land. "I have some money my Grandma Carter gave me when we left Ohio," she explained.

"How much do you have, Retta?" Gilson asked.

"Enough."

"Enough for a horse?" Christen challenged.

Joslyn flipped a buffalo chip over and brushed off some bugs with her hand before she dropped it in her sack. "Ansley MacGregor said her horse cost fifty dollars in St. Louis."

"Do you have fifty dollars, Retta?" Gilson asked.

"Of course not." Retta Barre marched ahead of the other girls as if playing Follow Me If You Dare. "I don't need a fine trotting horse. Just a common one will do."

"Like the pinto at the trading post?" Joslyn questioned. "I thought the man wanted twenty dollars for that horse."

"That was just the asking price. I'm sure he would have

negotiated," Retta insisted. "My brother Andrew paid only ten cash dollars for Beanie."

Gilson untied her calico bonnet and fanned her neck with her hand. "Do you have ten cash dollars, Retta?"

"No, but I don't need a horse as big as Beanie. Just a small pinto horse will do me fine, but he has to have nice colors. Chestnut and white would be good."

"How much do you have, Retta Barre?" Joslyn inquired.

"Six dollars," Retta muttered.

"You're going to buy a fancy horse like that for six dollars?" Joslyn challenged.

Retta licked her chapped lips. "Maybe I'll earn some more money."

"How're you going to do that?" Christen asked. "We're on a wagon train to Oregon City. You can't exactly make blackberry jam and sell it to old Mrs. Willington like you did in Barresville, Ohio."

"I'll think of something," Retta mumbled.

"Was your hometown really named after your kin?" Gilson asked.

"It was named after my grandfather," Retta replied.

"I don't think there was anything named after my family," Joslyn said. "I named a pet skunk after my brother once, but I don't suppose that counts."

Christen moved ahead of the others and picked up a buffalo chip for her sack. "Retta, I still say you won't be able to earn money on a wagon train."

Retta dug her heels into the soft sandy dirt. "I'll think of something."

"And buy a horse?" Christen said.

"Yes, I will."

"I don't think you can do it," Christen challenged.

Retta glanced at her slightly taller friend. "Is that a dare?"

A smile broke across Christen's face. "No. There is no one who dares Retta Barre."

Retta slipped her thumbs under the burlap strap of her sack to relieve the strain on her shoulder. "I'll have a pinto horse by the time we reach Fort Hall."

"How about Fort Bridger?" Joslyn asked. "Mama still says we may take the California cut-off there."

"I'll have a horse by the time we reach Independence Rock," Retta boasted.

"We'll be there in a week or so," Christen reminded her.

"Yes, well . . . I, eh, will have to get busy, won't I?" *Lord, why did I say that? Why do I say I'll do things I can't possibly accomplish?*

"Can I ride your horse, too, Retta?" Gilson asked. She coughed and dropped her sack. Then she added, "I love to ride horses."

"We can all take turns," Retta announced.

"And pile our chip sacks in the cart," Joslyn said giggling.

Retta stood up straight. "Oh, yes! A cart! Perhaps I will get a cart, too."

"By the time we get to Independence Rock?" Christen plodded next to her. "Now you're really dreaming, Retta Barre."

"But it's a nice dream," Joslyn remarked.

Gilson wiped her forehead on the sleeve of her light blue cotton dress. "My back hurts."

"Your back always hurts," Joslyn replied.

"I know. Doesn't your back ever hurt, Retta?"

"I guess not. My Papa says us Barres have strong bones."

Christen stared at her shadow stretching across the prairie. "My papa just says I'm fat."

"You're not fat. You just have big bones," Retta defended her.

Christen grinned. "I like that."

"Well, I'm not fat. I'm too skinny," Gilson confessed. "And I don't have strong bones. My shoulder really hurts."

"You've just been sick, Gilson. You have very pretty skin, you know. It's fair—just what the boys like. Look at me. I'm brown as dirt."

"I'm going to need to rest," Gilson said.

"I'll carry your bag for you," Retta offered.

"You can't carry two!" Gilson protested, but she didn't hesitate to hand her burlap bag to Retta.

Retta balanced a sack on each shoulder. "Oh? Who says?"

"I mean, I should carry my own," Gilson replied.

"You've just been a little poorly. When you get stronger and get over that cough, you'll be able to carry it," Retta assured her.

"She's been sick every day on the trail," Joslyn commented.

Retta gazed at the brown eyes of the shorter girl. "We all know that. Do you have a point to make, Joslyn?"

"Eh, no."

"I can't remember when I wasn't sick," Gilson admitted. "Papa says Oregon will make me well."

Retta watched the dust fog along the trail of wagons to the south. "Maybe we should go back now. Our sacks are nearly full."

"If we go back too soon, Mr. Landers will make me come back out for another load," Joslyn said.

Christen hiked up her ankle-length dress and tugged a burr from her white cotton stocking. "How come you always call your papa Mr. Landers?"

"He isn't my papa. He's my stepfather," Joslyn declared.

"But your papa is dead, and Mr. Landers is the only papa you're ever goin' to have," Christen said.

"He ain't my papa."

"It's okay," Retta put in. "Joslyn's mama calls him Mr. Landers, too."

"Yeah, Mama's that way. She's very polite," Joslyn confirmed.

"Do you want to hear what my mama calls my papa when the lamp is out and they think I'm asleep?" Christen smirked.

All four girls stopped hiking.

"What?" Retta pressed.

"Well . . . I don't know if I should tell you."

"What? What is it? What does he call her?" Joslyn bubbled.

"Promise you won't tell?" Christen urged.

"We promise! Tell us, tell us, tell us!" Gilson demanded.

"He calls her . . ."

The three girls held their breath in unison.

"'Peachy.'"

"What?" Gilson looked disappointed.

"In fact, he calls her 'Peachy dear.'"

Retta wrinkled her nose. "That's it?"

"Yes."

Joslyn shook her head. "I thought you were goin' to tell us something naughty."

"Joslyn Jouppi!" Christen exclaimed.

Retta picked up another chip and then caught up with them again. "Well, my papa calls my mama 'darlin'.'"

"Your papa calls ever' girl 'darlin','" Christen pointed out.

"And what's wrong with that?" Retta snapped.

"Nothing."

Gilson stopped and stared at a buffalo chip. "Retta, are you really going to get a horse before we reach Independence Rock?"

"Yes."

The girls walked in silence for several minutes. A fly buzzed around Retta's head, and she shook her thick brown hair back and forth to chase it off.

"You think we'll see a real, live grizzly bear?" Gilson asked. "I don't like bears."

"I heard Bobcat Bouchet say that the scariest thing he'd ever seen was Mrs. Mallory before she combed her hair in the mornings." Joslyn giggled.

"My papa says Mr. Bouchet tends to stretch the truth a little," Retta observed. "But in that case, he may be right."

Christen pointed to the wagon train. "Look who's coming out!"

"It's Ansley," Gilson said.

"And her fifty dollar horse," Christen mumbled.

Joslyn let her burlap bag slip to the ground, and she rubbed her shoulder. "How come Ansley MacGregor doesn't have to pick up chips with us?"

"Her daddy hired those two men to cook and gather chips," Retta replied.

Gilson brushed her blonde hair back over her shoulders and retied her bonnet. "I think Ansley is very pretty."

"Well, she is thirteen," Christen put in.

Gilson stood tall, her shoulders back. "Do you think I'll look like Ansley when I'm thirteen?"

"I don't think I'll look that good when I'm sixteen." Retta sighed.

"Lerryn is sixteen, and she's very pretty," Gilson encouraged her.

Retta watched as the girl rode straight for them.

"Lerryn looks like Mama. The boys look like Papa. I don't look like anybody."

"Your papa is very handsome. My mama said so," Gilson declared.

Retta studied the blonde-haired, blue-eyed girl. "She did? She said that?"

"She said, 'Mr. Barre is a very handsome man when he smiles, but he doesn't smile enough.'"

Retta turned and marched ahead of the others. "He smiles. He's just quite busy, you know. He has lots of worries on his mind."

As Retta tramped along, the soft prairie dirt sank under each foot. *Lord, sometimes I feel so out of place, even in my own family. There's Mama and Lerryn . . . and there's William, Andrew, and Papa . . . and then there's me. I'm like that extra fork at Aunt Clara's that nobody knows when to use. Not that I'm complaining. Okay, maybe I'm complaining a little.*

Two

A cloud of dust rolled over the four gingham-clad girls as red-haired Ansley MacGregor reined up beside them. She wore a leather skirt and a straw hat tilted to the side. The long-necked black horse pranced from side to side. His dark eyes darted toward the river.

"Have any of you little girls seen Benjamin Weaver?"

Christen held her hand to her forehead and shaded her eyes. "What do you want my brother for?"

Ansley studied the horizon. "I have a message for him."

"Tell me the message, and I'll tell him next time I see him," Christen offered.

Ansley cocked one thick red eyebrow. "I'm afraid it's much too delicate for you."

Gilson pointed a thin arm north. "He went over that hill and toward the river."

"Thank you. Ta-ta." Ansley laid her heels into the flanks of the black horse.

The girls waited for the dust to settle before they spoke.

"Ta-ta?" Joslyn mocked.

"Little girls?" Christen fumed.

Gilson untied her bonnet string. "What's a delicate message?" She coughed.

Retta grinned. "Something we're not supposed to hear."

"Why is she talking to your brother about delicate things?" Joslyn puzzled.

"I don't know," Christen answered. "I bet she made that up."

"I dreamed that Ansley's wagon sank completely out of sight in the quicksand."

"You did?" Gilson looked intrigued.

"Well, it wasn't really a night dream. I just sort of day-dreamed."

"Just because she called you a little girl last week?" Christen asked.

"And she rode through camp and kicked out our fire. And the time she borrowed my water scoop to use on her horse. And she told me if I got any more tan, I could be sold in Charleston. And she asked me not to sing around the camp-fire because I was messing up her concentration." Retta sucked in a deep breath and let it out slowly. "Should I go on?"

"Eh, I think we should change the subject," Christen proposed.

"Good. Who wants to race back to the wagons?" Retta challenged.

"Carrying chip sacks?" Joslyn objected.

"Sure."

"It wouldn't be fair. Retta's got two," Gilson pointed out.

"Are you saying I couldn't run with two sacks?"

"I'm saying you couldn't win, and that wouldn't be fair."

"I happen to have very sturdy legs."

"And strong bones." Christen giggled.

Joslyn adjusted her sack higher on her shoulder. "Okay, let's race."

"I'm not feeling too well," Gilson announced. "I don't think I'll run."

"You can count us down," Retta suggested.

Gilson stepped out in front of the girls. "Ready? Three . . . two . . . one . . . GO!" she yelled.

Burlap straps cut into Retta's shoulders as she sprinted across tableland prairie. Even in June the grass was clipped tight against the brown dirt by cattle that had grazed the trail ahead of them.

Retta spied Joslyn's dark hair and determined jaw to her right. Christen's brown curly hair bounced on her left.

I'm not going to lose even if I have to carry Gilson's sack, even if Christen has longer legs, even it takes my last breath of air. I'm not going to lose!

The line of wagons stretched across the blue horizon until they looked like nothing more than crude miniature replicas. They moved so slowly that only the Nebraska dust revealed their progress.

Retta felt her thigh muscles burn as she pushed her lace-up, high-top shoes into the dirt. First Joslyn, then Christen fell back, and soon she could see neither.

Don't turn around and look. I know I can win. I have fast legs. I am not fat, Travis Lott. I just have strong bones.

The pale blue prairie sky was faded like an abandoned robin's egg left out in the sun. Sharp pains shot through Retta's shoulders. The burlap rubbed through her dress and began to chafe her skin. Her mouth dropped open as she gasped for breath.

As she approached, the wagons grew gradually larger. The white canvas and red spokes were caked with yellow-brown dust, making the horizon look fuzzy, like when she first woke up after sleeping with her arm across her eyes.

To the left she spotted the green water barrel of Joslyn's wagon, and she knew that her wagon was two ahead of it. She slanted across the cropped slough grass and kept focused on the wagon with a yellow flap at the rear.

I told them I would win! I knew I could. And I have twice as much to carry!

She sprinted to the side of the six-ox wagon. She heard her father shout "Gee! Gee!" as he turned the team a little to the right. Now Retta could see her mother's bonnet and the white apron she wore over her blue calico dress. Panting, Retta pulled even with the front seat of the wagon.

"Hi, Mama!" she hollered. "I won!"

It could have been a hoof print or a small hole dug by previous wagon trains. It probably was a prairie dog hole. Whatever it was, Retta's right toe caught something, and she reached out to keep herself from landing face first in the dirt. One bag of buffalo chips tumbled across the prairie. The other folded under her, caught her in the stomach, and pinned her hand.

Her face smashed into the prairie soil. Retta rolled to her right, but she couldn't breathe.

"Are you all right, baby?" her mother called out as the wagon continued to roll.

Retta grabbed her chest but couldn't say anything.

The covered wagon kept its plodding pace. Her mother turned toward her. "I said, are you all right, baby?"

Retta nodded her head, still clutching her chest.

"Well, Coretta, stick those chips under the wagon while we're moving. Daddy doesn't want us to slow down."

Retta rolled over on her back. Air exploded back into her lungs. She gasped as if coming out of cold water after a dive into the river. Sweat rolled down her cheeks.

A buckskin gelding thundered up to her as she struggled to her feet.

"What are you doin' in the dirt, li'l sis?"

"I . . . was racing, and I . . . tripped at the finish line."

"Racing? You mean, it was a game?"

"Yes. And I won, William!"

"Who were you racing?"

"Christen, and Joslyn, and Gilson . . . well, not Gilson. She doesn't feel good, but—"

"They are all walking."

Retta spun around. Her three friends on the horizon sauntered toward the wagon train. "We were racing, but I was going to beat them, and so they must have quit."

"Well, don't be runnin' up to the train like that and fallin' down," William cautioned. "I thought you had spotted Indians or somethin'."

"I didn't see any Indians!" she reported.

William waved his arm at her. "Okay, pick up that mess."

"I really won," she insisted.

"There was nobody runnin' but you, Coretta Emily!" William laughed and then rode back toward the lead wagon.

"Are you all right, girl?" Mr. O'Day called out as his wagon rolled near.

"Yes," Retta said. "I stepped in a prairie dog hole. One of these chip sacks is Gilson's."

"Load it up while we're movin'," he ordered. "Them sacks don't look very full."

"They were getting kind of heavy," she explained. Retta took the full sack and jogged alongside the plodding wagon, tossing the buffalo chips on the canvas sling suspended under the box, between the axles of the wagon. Then she trudged back to the other sack and picked up the spilled buffalo chips. She had just finished when her three friends reached her.

"I won!" Retta hollered.

Joslyn shrugged. "You won."

"How come you quit?" Retta asked.

"I was tired," Christen replied.

"So was I, but I don't quit just because I'm tired," Retta huffed.

"I was too tired to even begin," Gilson said.

"Well, anyway, I won!" Retta boasted. "I told you I could run with two sacks."

"I wonder if you could run with four sacks?" Joslyn pondered.

Three girls laughed.

"Maybe our bones aren't as strong as yours," Christen remarked.

William soon took over the ox-driving chore. Retta saw her father ride off toward the river as she brushed off her dress. She rummaged through the green chest and found some camphor salve to rub on her skinned elbow. Then she climbed up on the back of the slow-moving wagon to see if the butter had churned as it bounced on the tailgate. She heard her mother say something to Colonel Lancelot Graves, but he was riding on down the line by the time she crawled up into the seat. "Mama, what did the colonel say?"

Mrs. Barre handed Retta the corner of her apron. "We will be stopping soon. You have a smudge on your cheek, baby."

Retta wiped her face. "Stop for the night? But there's still plenty of daylight to burn."

"You're beginning to sound like your father. The colonel said we'd park in a straight line and pitch the tents to the southwest. He's expecting a storm and said this higher ground would be a good place to stop."

"Storm? A real storm? With clouds and everything?"

"That's what a storm usually means."

"But it's been real still all day."

"That's what worries the colonel. Bobcat Bouchet says there's a lightning storm coming this way."

"But there aren't even any clouds," Retta protested. She scanned the flat western horizon. "Except that little one."

Mrs. Barre fanned herself with a small paper fan. She rubbed the small of her back and then tried to smooth her apron across her stomach. "This weather is different from back home. It just explodes on us all at once out here. Go tell your sister to come back to our wagon. We'll need to make things watertight."

"Where is Lerryn?" Retta asked.

"Where do you think?"

"Visiting with Nancy Suetter, I suppose."

"She and Nancy are very good friends."

"That's only because of Brian Suetter."

"Brian's out with the cattle," her mother said. "At least, I think he is."

"After I find Lerryn, can I go tell Daddy and Andrew?"

Mrs. Barre studied the northern horizon. "Baby, with the rise in the prairie, I can't even see the river from here. This is a strange land. At home we can't see the river for the trees. Out here there are no trees, and we still can't see the river. Yes, you go tell them, but don't go by yourself. You know how worried I can get. I'm afraid I don't have the patience out here, baby."

"Mama, I'm really not a baby."

Mrs. Barre grinned. "Coretta Emily, I won't be able to call you that much longer, I know. Just humor me awhile longer. Now tell Papa that the colonel said to bunch the cattle and guard them close. If there's lightning, they might run off."

Retta's blue eyes widened. "I've never seen a stampede before! I wonder if we'll see St. Elmo's fire dancing off the horns and their wild red eyes flashing and horns rattling, and the thunder of destruction will be forever logged in our minds."

"You've been reading those penny-press books again!"

"Just one, Mama—*The Calico Queen of West Texas*."

"Well, purple-gingham queen, go find your sis."

"It's pansy plum, Mama." Retta hopped down and trotted along the wagons behind them. A big, bearded man screamed "Haw!" and turned his oxen a little to the left. She waited until he cracked his whip above the oxen's heads. "Mr. O'Day, is Gilson in the wagon?"

"She's takin' a nap, girl," he bellowed. "Don't you go botherin' her."

Retta ran to another wagon. "Mrs. Jouppi—I mean Mrs. Landers, is Joslyn here?"

The tiny woman with coal-black hair peered out from under her bonnet. "I thought she was with you. She must be in Christen's wagon."

Retta glanced up and down the wagon train. *I wonder why they didn't come get me? Maybe I'll just go out and find Papa and Andrew on my own. I know my way around better than the boys do!*

Retta tramped across the dirt toward the river and then spun around. *Lerryn! Why do I always have to fetch my sister? She's four years older. She ought to fetch herself.*

Retta stomped back down the line of wagons until she reached the one with dusty fringed curtains. A very tall man hiked alongside the oxen. His eyes were almost closed. He looked half-asleep.

"Hi, Mr. Suetter."

The man threw his shoulders back and blinked open his eyes. "Eh . . . hello, young Miss Barre. I think I was dreaming of Oregon."

"I do that all the time, Mr. Suetter."

"How are you today?"

"I'd be better if I were riding a horse."

The tall man laughed and cracked the whip above the lead ox. "Wouldn't we all? You lookin' for your sis?"

"Yes, sir."

"She's at the back of the wagon, I think."

Retta stood by the side of the wagon and waited for it to roll past her. A boy and a girl were sitting at the back, their legs trailing over the tailgate.

"Were you spying on me?" Lerryn called out as Retta approached.

"No, I wasn't. Mama sent me to fetch you."

"What for?"

"She wants you to help set up a watertight camp. The colonel said a storm is coming."

"There's no storm coming today," Lerryn argued.

"The colonel said it was."

Lerryn leaned her shoulder against Brian Suetter's. "You're making up this story just to get me to go back to the wagon."

"Why would I do that? I don't care what you do. But Mama wants you at the wagon."

Brian Suetter jumped off the wagon and helped Lerryn get down. "I heard the same thing. Maybe you'd better go. I don't want your mama mad at me."

"Mama thinks Lerryn is with your sister."

"Then I especially don't want her mad at me!"

"You'd better be telling me the truth!" Lerryn huffed.

"I'll walk you to your wagon," Brian offered.

"Mama thinks you're out tending cattle," Retta cautioned.

"In that case, maybe I shouldn't walk you back." Brian Suetter's smile revealed two deep dimples.

"I'm going to the river to tell Papa and Andrew about the storm," Retta announced.

"By yourself?" Brian asked.

"You can come with me if you want."

The tall, broad-shouldered young man glanced at Lerryn and then back at Retta. "I guess I'd better not, li'l sis."

"That's okay. I just said that to see the frown on Lerryn's face."

Lerryn turned away from Brian and stuck out her tongue. Then she spun around. "You could walk with me for a while," she cooed. "Mama can't see around the corner."

"I reckon I could at that." He grinned.

Retta stood still as the wagon train continued to roll past her.

I don't need anyone to go with me. Papa is right over that rise. Besides, they are all tired. We've been gone two long months, and everyone is tired.

Retta Barre plowed her way across the prairie toward the rise and the unseen river beyond.

Lord, this is the grandest adventure of my life, and it's kind of boring. One straight line . . . sixty wagons, eleven men on horseback, and a two-wheeled cart. Roll twelve miles west—then camp for the night. It takes us ten or twelve hours. I can walk it in three. I wish I had a horse to ride.

If I had a horse, I could ride with the wind like Ansley. And my hair would flag out, and the boys would look at me, and they would . . .

Okay. Even with a horse, no one would notice me.

I don't care.

I still really wish I had a horse to ride.

Three

By the time Retta reached the top of the rolling knoll north of the wagon train, the far western sky was cluttered with a flotilla of dark clouds, and her mind was jumbled with thoughts. She paused and looked back.

Lord, I know that we're doing something special. Papa says we're creating history. William says that someday steam trains will take people clear to Oregon City and Sacramento. We'll be a part of the past. But, Lord, I didn't know history could be so slow, so dull. Every day is just like the one before, except that the flies and gnats are getting worse. If I have to write in my diary about buffalo chips one more time, I'll scream. I think maybe a little more excitement would make better history, don't You?

To the north wispy, tall slough grass marked the wide river's edge. She spied the black and white milk cows and extra oxen and the outline of a man on horseback. She hiked straight at the man. When he spotted her approach, he turned and rode toward her.

"Darlin', what are you doin' out here by yourself?"

"Papa, Colonel Graves warned that a serious storm is moving in fast, and he's stopping us for the night. He's calling in the cattle and horses."

Mr. Barre stood in the ox-bow stirrups of his centerfire saddle. He pulled his red bandanna from his pocket and wiped his forehead. "I've been watchin' those clouds myself. I'll ride over and tell Andrew. We'll move them back. You want to ride with me?"

Retta scooted around to her father's left side. "Oh, yes!" She dropped her chin. "Of course, if I had my own horse, I could help you, and Prince wouldn't have to carry two."

He wiped his forehead again and sat back in the saddle. "Not many girls have their own horses. Your mama is dead set against it, but I'll try to soften her, darlin'. Maybe when we get to Oregon."

The sun was now blocked by the western clouds, but she shaded her eyes with her hand anyway. "Ansley has her own horse."

"Darlin', the MacGregors have quite a bit of everything. Most of the young boys on this wagon train don't even have a horse of their own. I saw Ben Weaver out walkin' a little while ago. Ben doesn't have a horse."

She stared at the tall grass by the river. "Did he turn back to the wagons?"

Mr. Barre pointed to the northwest. "No, he was checkin' out that brush up there."

Retta couldn't see anything but the banks of the river and thick brush with light green leaves. "I think they lost a cow."

"Really? Mr. Weaver never told me about that."

"Maybe I should go tell Ben to turn back before the storm hits," she suggested.

"Okay, darlin'. Hurry up and then come on back and ride with me. Andrew and I will graze this bunch back to the wagons. You can catch up with us . . . unless you want to walk back with young Benjamin."

"Papa!"

"Now, darlin', your papa knows your heart. You know that, don't you?"

"I know, Papa! But I want to ride with you."

She hiked past the cattle. Just as she reached the thickest part of the brush, Retta stopped and picked up a stick. It was almost as tall as she was and at least two inches thick. The bark had been peeled off, and there were two horizontal grooves sliced into it.

Someone has lost a perfectly good walking stick. I wonder if it was from my wagon train . . . or maybe one that is ahead of us. This is a very good coyote stick. If one comes close to me, I'll teach it some respect, I will.

Retta used the stick to shove aside the brush and crawl through toward the water's edge. The North Platte River was about one hundred yards across and looked shallow. She studied its winding course.

It's in no more of a hurry than my wagon train. Nothing out on the plains is in a hurry . . . unless it's those clouds. She swatted a mosquito on her forehead. *And the bugs!*

Within minutes the prairie sky was half-filled with swirling dark clouds. The winds stirred up dust even in the brush beside the river.

I don't see Ben . . . or a cow. I can't see much at all with this dirt in my eyes. I don't think he lost a cow anyway. He just wanted to get away so he wouldn't have to pick up buffalo dung. But he didn't make it. I won. I won, Ben Weaver! No matter how cute your smile is and how much you ignore me, I won! So there. And you can find your own way back to the wagon train.

The thick brush ahead of her rustled with sticky dark green leaves. She jabbed the tall stick once again to open a hole and plunge through. The wind blasted her face as she fought her way through the tangled brush. Several times she stooped to shove past limbs. When she finally came out of the brush, she could not see her father, brother, or the cattle.

Retta hiked up to the knoll. Clouds now covered the entire sky. She felt the sting of blown dust. When she reached the crest, she squinted at what she thought was southwest. Her heart leaped. She grabbed her chest with her hand and clutched the stick.

"It's gone!" she blurted out. "The whole wagon train is gone!" *It can't be gone. They were going to stop. They have to be right there. Unless . . . unless I got turned around.*

They can't leave me!

Where are they?

Lord, this is definitely not the adventure I was looking for.

Retta took a deep breath and held it as she clamped her lips tight. Then she puffed out her cheeks.

I am not lost! Retta Barre does not get lost. I am not frightened, and I will not cry. I'm sure the wagon train is just over that next rise.

Even though the wind was at her back, she dropped her chin to her chest and squinted her eyes, the tall walking stick thrust in front of her like a club. At the top of the next dusty knoll, she stared down on an empty sea of brown grass.

She puffed out her cheeks again and bit her lip. *I am not lost. They must have raced on to a good camping spot. Maybe the colonel decided to go off the trail. Maybe they're camped by the river after all. It would be better to camp there. I'll just hike . . .*

She spun around to face the sting of the wind.

The wind is coming from the west, and I was hiking east. That's the problem. I just got turned around in that brush. I'll go into the wind.

Retta tramped straight west, her hand across her forehead to block the wind from her eyes. The other hand dragged the stick alongside her.

Papa will be worried sick. He'll be going up and down the river. I'll just stay down there until Andrew or Papa comes by. I hope it's Papa. I didn't cross the river, and I'm headed west, so that's the right direction.

Retta Barre doesn't get lost.

It's all your fault, Ben Weaver. I didn't have to go look for you. I wonder if he's lost? It serves him right. I'll probably have to rescue him.

The sky darkened as if the sun had set. Thunder rolled from some place to the north.

The rain will settle the dust. That will be good. I do hope Mama feels like cooking a hot meal tonight. She's been sick too much. If it gets too wet, we'll have a cold supper. My clothes will be very, very dirty. I need to comb the dirt out of my hair. Hah, it's good that it's me out here and not Lerryn. She would cry because her precious wavy hair is messed up. Well, there's something good about thick, short, straight hair. I can comb it fast and not worry about it.

When she reached the next rise in the prairie, she stared into the wind. There was nothing in sight.

No cattle.

No wagons.

No river.

I am not lost! The river is to the north. I'm swerving to the south. I'll walk north until I get to the river and then go west. I know my way around. Papa says I have a very good sense of direction.

He also says I don't have much discretion. Why does he always have to be right?

As thunder boomed closer, clouds lowered, and the wind died down. She felt a sprinkle or two on her face.

I will show up at the wagon looking like a wet dog, and Mama will make me change clothes. She'll probably make me go straight to bed and hang my clothes in the wagon to dry. I might not even get any supper.

I wish I were in bed right now.

She crested a knoll and still could not see the river.

I am not scared.

She puffed out her cheeks again and pressed her lips tighter.

Lord, I might be just a little bit scared. Please help me.

The thunder closed in on her. Lightning flashes danced on the dirt west of her. When she reached the next knoll, she saw a line of tall brush only a hundred yards ahead of her.

See! I can find my way around. There's the river! Thank You, Lord. I'll follow it into the wind and be there shortly.

"Where have you been, darlin'?" Papa will say.

"I was looking for that Weaver boy like you asked me to. What's the matter with boys? Can't they find their way on their own?"

And he will laugh and tousle my hair and wink at me.

Lord, my papa has the nicest wink in the whole world. Do you ever wink, Lord? Maybe You are winking at me now!

Retta turned west and trudged into the wind and light rain as she shoved her way through the brush next to the river.

The sky darkened. She continued to push upstream. The raindrops trickled down her forehead and cheeks. She rubbed her neck and brought away dirty fingers. The wet brush now smeared her face and pansy-plum dress like a paintbrush. She popped out into a clearing no bigger than a chicken yard. "I'm a mess, Lord," she hollered into the storm. "But I'm not lost."

There was a whimper, a cry.

But it wasn't hers.

The young voice sent a cold flash down Retta's back. She spun around and raised the stick above her head.

A small boy in deerskin trousers, with long black hair halfway down his bare brown back, sprawled in the brush, clutching his foot.

An Indian!

He screamed in terror.

But Retta couldn't hear him. She was screaming even louder.

At the same moment lightning flashed, and thunder exploded over the river. For a split second, both of them stared at the storm.

Then Retta screamed and dove back into the brush. She stumbled and turned around. "You get away from me!" she hollered.

But the boy was dragging his injured leg, clawing his way across the riverbank trying to get away from her.

Retta lowered the stick. *He's as scared as I am. He looks terrified. Of me? How can an Indian be scared of me?* She stepped closer and squinted her eyes. *A real Indian. Up close. He's just a little boy, but he's an Indian! I win! I'm the first one in our wagon train to see an Indian up close!*

He tried to crawl back into the brush.

Retta scratched her head above her ear. "Did you hurt yourself?"

Tears tracked across his dusty face. He picked up a rock as if to throw it at her.

Retta held up her hands. "No! I won't hurt you. Do you need some help?" She stepped closer.

He didn't back away but pointed to the stick, shouted some words, and then pointed at his chest.

"This is your stick? It's a very nice stick."

Retta handed the boy the stick. He grabbed it and clutched it with both hands. She watched as he struggled to use the stick as a crutch and pull himself to his feet.

"I can help you if you want," she offered again.

The minute he put weight on the injured foot, he collapsed in tears.

She walked very slowly toward the boy. Her voice was soft, almost drowned by the now-distant thunder. "Let me help you. Where is your home? I didn't see any tepees or cabins or anything." She squatted down beside him. "Here, put your arm on my shoulder."

She took his hand.

He didn't pull away.

The grip was wet, sticky, and hesitant.

Retta pointed to the stick. "Hold that in one hand. Lean on me with the other. Let's stand up."

Slowly she got the boy to his feet.

"Now which way? Where is your family?"

The boy hung his chin on his chest.

"Oh, are you embarrassed because you twisted your ankle? You know, I fell down today myself. Right in front of my mother. Everyone in the wagon train has heard about it by now." She stared west into the storm. "Should we go this way?"

The boy sniffed, then nodded.

The rain increased, and Retta felt her dress get wetter as they limped through the brush next to the river.

Lord, I don't even know what Indians like to talk about. What am I supposed to say? "Like I said, I fell down and hurt my ankle a little, but I had on these nice shoes. Well, they were nice when we left Ohio. I guess they look rather worn now." Retta glanced down at the boy's bare feet. "Perhaps shoes don't impress you."

She thought the boy was walking a little better.

"Did I scare you? We sort of scared each other, and then the lightning scared us both. Funny how one thing that seems quite scary is suddenly put in its place. I talk a lot when I'm nervous. And I'm really, really nervous. You see, you're the first Indian I've . . . I've, eh, touched. And you don't understand a word I'm saying, do you?"

She noticed the rain trickle down the boy's brown chest.

"You really shouldn't be out in a storm without a shirt on. Oh, dear, I don't even know if you have a shirt. I guess your mother knows best. But that's the way mothers are. My mother's been feeling poorly for several months. Do Indians ever get sick?"

Even though he walked considerably better, he continued to lean on Retta's shoulder.

She reached up and patted his hand. Then he patted hers back. "I don't even know your name. My real name is Coretta Emily Barre, but everyone calls me Retta, except Mama. Papa usually calls me 'darlin'.' What's your name?"

The boy pointed to Retta and let out an excited string of unfamiliar words.

Lord, this conversation is about as exciting as a wagon train ride. Neither of us knows anything the other is saying. But I did get to meet a real Indian! If we can't find his family, I'll take him back to the wagon train. Maybe Mr. Bouchet can speak to him. "Retta Barre brought a real Indian to camp." *Even Ansley MacGregor hasn't done that.*

The brush thickened as the riverbank grew steeper. The leaves of the brush continued to soak their faces. When she broke through the brush, the river bed turned abruptly north, leaving a huge sandstone cave gouged out in the riverbank. It was sheltered from the wind and completely invisible from the wagon train's side of the prairie.

And it was full of people.

All with brown skin and long black hair.

All wearing buckskin.

Retta held her breath and puffed out her cheeks.

I don't think I'm supposed to be here!

Four

*A*man with a red bandanna tied around his forehead ran out and grabbed the boy's shoulder. "Hurry!" he shouted to her. "It is a bad storm! There is room for you with us."

Retta shook her head. *I am not scared!*

A woman with a baby in her arms stepped out into the rain. She approached and reached for Retta's hand. The baby started to cry as the rain pelted its little brown face.

Retta felt the rain trickle down the back of her dress. Thunder and lightning crashed behind her. She spun around to see the sky light up like at noon and then go dark. She clutched the woman's wet, warm hand.

In the sandstone cave, Retta huddled next to the woman, who sat down on a bundle and returned to nursing the baby. At first Retta stared straight out at the storm and didn't move a muscle.

The man who spoke English and an old woman were examining the boy's foot. The old woman rubbed a black tar-like substance on the boy's ankle.

I don't want to be here, Lord. This isn't my place. This is a bad dream. I want to wake up and hear Lerryn snore. I want to pull my quilt over my head and hide until we get to Oregon.

Her eyes began to adjust to the darkness of the cave,

and she allowed her gaze to wander. The sandstone sloped to a narrow crevice in the back. The floor was deep, fine sand. Along one wall she saw long lodge poles, deer-hide wrapped bundles, buffalo robes, a very large cast-iron pot, and some pottery jugs. She spotted three boys, two girls, a very old woman, two young men, and the woman with the baby. And at least seven horses.

She refused to stare at the people, most of whom were staring at her. She did look at the horses.

The storm was so dark she could hardly see all of their faces until the lightning flashed. Her dress hung wet and heavy, and she felt cold.

The man with the bandanna stepped up to her. "Bear Heart thanks you for helping him. I believe he got lost in the sudden storm and hurt his ankle."

Retta nodded her head. *Lord, I don't know how to talk to Indians. Please, Lord, don't let them scalp me. These are . . . these are wild savages! But, well, they don't look too wild.*

"I am sorry we have no fire yet. This storm came up very fast," the man said. "We will build one right away."

Retta puffed out her cheeks.

He leaned close and stared at her face. "You are surprised I speak English?"

Retta nodded.

One of the young men stepped up to a bundle and pulled out a strip of dried meat. He bit off a piece and then held it toward her.

"Are you hungry?" the man next to her asked.

"No," she managed to murmur. "No, thank you."

"My name is Two Bears." The man pointed back at the others. "This my family."

"My name is Retta Emily Barre. I'm twelve years old and from Barresville, Ohio. I'm on the covered wagon train going to Oregon City, Oregon, and I need to get back to my papa before he gets worried and comes looking for me with a gun!" she blurted out.

"Your name is Bear?" The man rubbed his smooth brown chin.

"Yes, Retta Barre."

Two Bears spoke rapidly to the others in a language she had never heard. Then everyone laughed.

"What did you say to them?" she murmured. "Are they laughing at me?"

"I merely said that your name is also Bear. I said that because you don't have sickly white skin like the others, perhaps we are relatives."

"My name is spelled . . ." Retta looked at everyone staring at her every word. "Eh, maybe we are relatives."

"Yes!" the man beamed. "I knew when I first saw you helping Bear Heart that you were one of us."

The woman with the infant sat on one of the deerskin bundles and rocked the baby back and forth. The old woman carved splinters off a dry stick. Rain poured hard outside the opening of the cave, and the sky was almost black.

Bear Heart hobbled over to Two Bears and said something.

"You belong to the wagon with the yellow canvas door?" Two Bears inquired.

"You have seen my wagon?" Retta folded her arms across her chest. "Have you been spying on us?"

The man's face was expressionless as he stared out at the dark rain. "We have watched all the wagons."

"But I didn't see you. Nobody saw you. How long have you watched my wagon?"

"We have watched them all for fifteen days," Two Bears reported.

"But I didn't know you were here."

"We were afraid you might shoot at us if we approached," Two Bears explained.

Retta could feel the wet dress hang on her shoulders. "I don't even have a gun!"

They whispered something among themselves.

"But my papa has a gun!" she added quickly.

Two Bears squatted on his haunches beside her at the mouth of the cave. "Thank you for helping Bear Heart. He said you found his horse stick. That's why he was out there. He lost his horse stick and was hunting for it."

"What is a horse stick?"

"I gave that to him when he was only four years old and wanted his own horse. I told him he had to wait until he was as tall as that stick to have his own horse."

Retta folded her arms across her damp dress. "I'm taller than that stick!"

"Do you have your own horse?" he asked.

She studied the woman and the round-faced baby. "No, but I want one very, very much. I saw a beautiful one back at the trading post near Scotts Bluff. But I didn't have enough money. Besides, my mother says it's not ladylike for a girl to ride a horse. But Papa says when I save enough money, I can buy a horse. One that he approves, of course. But I'll never have enough money."

Two Bears drew his fingers through the dry sand in the cave. "Then you should trade for one."

Retta squatted beside the man in buckskin. "Yes, I should! But what could I trade for a pony?"

"That depends."

"On what?"

"On the pony. What do you have to trade?" he asked.

"That depends," she grinned, "on the pony."

He said something to the others, and they laughed.

The young man at the side with the horses shouted out something.

Two Bears smiled, revealing large, straight white teeth. "Brown Bear says he is sure that you are a relative!"

He stood up and so did Retta.

"You speak very good English," she said.

"Thank you. I was a tracker for old man Bridger."

"Jim Bridger?"

"Yes. Do you know him?"

"Oh, no. But I read this book about him. It was a penny novel actually, but don't tell my mother."

"I will not tell her. Does your mother look like you?"

"Oh, no, I don't look like anyone in my family!"

"Perhaps you are in the wrong family. I believe you look like my wife's younger sister."

"Really?"

"Yes, do you speak Shoshone?"

"No!" she grinned.

Two Bears cracked a smile. "I taught Bridger Shoshone, and he taught me English."

One of the girls spoke to the woman with the baby. She in turn spoke to the man.

"My wife, Lucy, says you have a very pretty dress."

Retta glanced down at her wet, dirty dress. "Tell her thank you very much." She studied the gray streaks in the woman's waist-length black hair. "Your wife's name is Lucy?"

"Lucy Two Bears. It is a nice name, don't you think?"

"Yes, it is. Lucy Two Bears. It's a wonderful name. Your wife has very beautiful hair."

He said something to his wife, and she smiled as she rocked the baby back and forth.

Retta smelled unwashed bodies and horse manure.

"My first name is really Coretta, but I hate that name. Everyone calls me Retta. Everyone except Mama."

"What does she call you?" the man asked.

"She calls me 'baby' 'cause I'm the youngest child."

Two Bears translated her words to the others. "Retta Bear. I like that name." He rubbed his clean-shaven chin. "From now on we will call you 'Red Bear.'"

"But my name is . . ." Retta paused.

He said something to the others, and she saw them nodding approval.

She rocked back on her heels. "Yes, I like that. I shall be 'Red Bear'! But I don't have red hair."

The man grinned. "And I don't have two bears."

On her hands and knees in the cave, the old woman gathered up the splinters she had whittled, bunched them in a pile, and struck a flint against a rock. A spark ignited the shavings, and soon a smoky fire started. The old woman and the two girls dug out supplies from one of the bundles.

"You will stay and eat with us?"

Retta stepped out of the cave and held her palms up. "The rain is slowing down. I should find my papa before he gets worried and comes looking for me."

"You mean, before he comes looking for you with a gun?" Two Bears added.

The two young men in buckskin trousers led the horses out of the cave and into the brush beside the river. Bear Heart drew a circle in the dirt with his horse stick. He and another boy began to play a game with small, round white pebbles they held in each hand.

"I will have Shy Bear show you the way back to the wagons," Two Bears announced.

The woman finished nursing her baby, and a girl about Retta's age took the baby and bounced him on her hip. She spoke to the woman, who then spoke to the man.

"This is our daughter, Shy Bear," Two Bears announced.

"Her name is Shy?"

"She has a beautiful smile," Two Bears declared.

"Yes, she does," Retta agreed.

"She wants to trade you."

Retta glanced down at her empty hands.

Shy Bear rested her chin on her chest and stared at the dirt.

"She wants to trade her dress for your dress," Two Bears explained.

"She does?" Retta studied the girl's buckskin dress with blue glass beads on the fringe. "But—but her dress is beautiful, and mine is so plain."

"She has always wanted a purple dress."

Retta folded her arms across her chest. "But this dress is not very new, and it's really not purple; it's pansy plum." She stared into Two Bears's eyes. "Would it be a fair trade?"

He put one hand on her shoulder and the other on Shy Bear's shoulder. "If she is happy, and you are happy, it is a good trade."

Retta felt some warmth blaze from the small fire. The cave filled with wispy smoke. "Maybe she could come back with me to my wagon, and I'll ask my mother. Perhaps she'll let me trade."

Two Bears dropped his hands to his side. "No, I won't let my daughter go with you. I don't know your people. She could get hurt. She is afraid of those on the wagon train. She is afraid she will be captured and made into a slave."

Retta rubbed her round nose with the palm of her hand. "She's afraid of us?"

"Sometimes people on wagon trains shoot at us without talking to us."

Lord, everyone on the wagons is afraid of Indians. And the Indians are afraid of us? We aren't very scary . . . are we? "I could make sure no one shoots at her."

"Does the pansy-plum dress belong to you or someone else?" he asked.

Retta tried to brush dirt off one sleeve. "Oh, it's my dress."

Lucy Two Bears said something to him. He shook his head.

"Do you have another dress, or is this your only one?" he asked.

Retta bit her lip and then blurted out, "I have four dresses, but one is in Mama's trunk. I can't wear it until we get to Oregon City."

The girl said a few words and pointed at Retta, giggling.

"Shy Bear wants to trade you right now," he said.

"H-here? In the cave? Switch dresses?" Retta stammered.

"Yes."

"But I—I need—I can't . . ."

"Red Bear, do you want to trade for the buckskin dress or not?" His voice was firm, not harsh.

"Yes, but I . . ."

He spoke to the girl. She shrieked and then laughed and danced around the smoky fire.

Retta stared at everyone watching her. *Lord, I have been scared to death to see Indians, and now I'm not scared at all. I know I should ask Mama first, but I don't think trading a dress is sinful . . . is it?*

"Okay, I'll trade," Retta announced. "But I still think her dress is much better than mine."

Two Bears spoke to Shy Bear. The girl immediately pulled off her dress. She wore nothing under it.

"Oh no, I can't—I can't . . . ," Retta mumbled and closed her eyes.

Two Bears studied her and then spoke to the others. They broke out in laughter, and all turned their backs to Retta.

"We will not look. My wife says perhaps you should be called 'Shy Red Bear.'"

I can't believe I'm doing this! I won't even let Lerryn watch when I change clothes! Lord, smite their eyes if they try to peek.

Shy Bear stood next to her, holding the buckskin dress. Retta pulled off her gingham and brushed down her camisole and bloomers. She quickly grabbed the buckskin. Before she pulled it over her head, Shy Bear was wearing the gingham. The Indian girl hopped around the cave, laughing and dancing. The whole family shouted and applauded.

Retta patted the pale buckskin dress with blue beads. *I didn't know it would be so soft! This is the prettiest dress I ever saw in my life!*

Shy Bear ran up to her and jabbered something.

Two Bears hugged his daughter. "She says to thank you for trading with her, Red Bear. This is the prettiest dress she has ever seen in her life."

Retta stared at the girl's dancing brown eyes.

Lord, I wish we could talk to each other. I bet Shy Bear and I would be really good friends.

"Do you like your dress?" Two Bears asked.

"Oh, yes! I love it. It's so soft."

"Lucy Two Bears chewed that hide soft."

Lord, I don't know what he meant by that, and I don't think I want to know. "It's a beautiful dress, and it fits me very well."

"Then you are both happy. It is a good trade indeed."

Retta glanced out at the drizzle. "I need to get back to my wagon now."

"Yes, you must hurry. There will be more rain soon," Two Bears agreed. "I'll have Shy Bear lead you there."

"Thank you!"

He spoke, and the girl walked out to the muddy ground. She motioned Retta to follow.

"Will you come to visit us again, Red Bear?" Two Bears asked.

"I would like to very much, but we're going to Oregon. I will be on down the trail."

"It will rain hard tonight. The wagons will be stuck for several days," Two Bears announced.

"Oh, no, we don't stop for anything. I'm sure we'll go on."

Two Bears smiled. "If you are stuck, come visit us."

"If my father will let me, I'll come back."

The little boy said something to his father.

"Bear Heart asks what happened to your hair?"

"What's wrong with my hair?"

"For a girl your age, it is short. He asks if you got it near the fire."

"It's not short. It almost comes to my shoulder, see?" She leaned her head to the side. "I just like short hair," she declared.

The old woman put more sticks on the fire and said something that made everyone laugh.

"What did she say?"

"My wife's mother said you will never get a husband with short hair."

"A husband? I don't even have a boyfriend!" *Oh. I was supposed to be looking for Ben!* "When I came down here, I was looking for a friend—a boy who is taller than me, with blond hair and a blue shirt. Did you see him?"

The man nodded and waved his hand to the west. "Yes. He rode off with the red-haired girl."

"Ansley? He rode on the black horse with Ansley MacGregor?"

The man raised his thick black eyebrows. "Did she steal your man?"

"My man? No! I'm only twelve," she protested.

He said something to the others, and they all laughed again. Then the old woman made a remark.

Two Bears grinned. "She said the girl on the black horse had long hair. She will get a husband soon."

"Well, I don't care who he rode with."

"Your lips are convincing, but your eyes betray you."

"If I had a horse, perhaps it would be different," she murmured.

"The horse at the trading post?"

"Yes. That would impress him."

"The horse?"

"No," she grinned. "Ben Weaver."

"Perhaps you should go back and get that horse."

"I can't. We're going west. And I need to get to my wagon now."

"Follow Shy Bear."

Retta tramped through the mud along the river, following the girl in the pansy-plum gingham dress. Neither spoke. Lightning flashed. Thunder rolled in the west, but it didn't rain anymore. From their position down the embankment next to the river, she couldn't see the wagon train as they hiked upstream. Retta's legs ached as she jogged to keep up with the shorter girl.

Finally Shy Bear stopped. She pointed up the embankment.

"Is the wagon train up there?"

The girl pointed again.

"Okay. Well . . . thank you, Shy Bear."

Shy Bear spoke several words. The only ones Retta understood were "Red Bear." Retta trudged to the top of the embankment and peered out on the stormy prairie.

There it is. The wagon train! And my wagon. Shy Bear brought me even with my wagon!

She spun around and stared back at the river, but she couldn't see anyone. She started to jog toward the wagon, but the mud on her shoes slowed her down. She slowed to a plod. As she approached the wagons, she heard someone blow the bugle and shout.

Retta stopped to look up and down the long line of covered wagons. *It's either time for a meeting, or there's trouble.*

Several men hiked out from the wagons with guns pointed. She could see people peering around the wagons at her.

"Stop right there and identify yourself!" Bobcat Bouchet shouted.

"I'm Retta Barre, and that is my wagon, Mr. Bouchet!" she yelled.

A man with a gun looped over his arm jogged out to her. "Retta darlin', are you all right?" he hollered as he approached.

"Hi, Papa! I took shelter in a cave along the river just like you taught me. And I met a very nice family of Indians."

"Retta, are you all right?" he repeated.

"And this girl named Shy Bear wanted to trade me dresses, so I just up and traded her."

"Retta darlin', did you hear me? I asked if you are all right," Mr. Barre repeated.

"They are a very nice family, and they took care of

me during the storm. Two Bears used to track for Jim Bridger."

Mr. Barre dropped to his knees and grabbed her shoulders. His face was only inches from hers. "Darlin', answer me!"

Retta threw her arms around his neck and kissed his rough cheek. "Yes, Daddy, I'm all right."

five

Christen's wet, curly bangs sagged down to her eyes. "Retta, how many Indians did you see?"

"Ten or twelve." Retta rocked back and forth on her heels as everyone crowded around her. "It was just one family really. They were all relatives."

Travis Lott's Adam's apple pulsed with every word. "Did they try to scalp you?"

Retta tugged her thick brown hair straight up. "Nope. It's all here. My hair has always been this short. But they were very nice. They let me stay with them out of the thunderstorm."

Joslyn's black parasol matched her hair. "Did they have red skin?"

"No, it was brown." In the distance Retta noticed some men ride off toward the river.

Gilson wrapped a gray wool blanket around her shoulders. She coughed a little and then cleared her throat. "Were they funny-looking?"

Retta rubbed her nose and rolled her eyes. "Eh . . . one was sort of funny-looking."

"What did he look like?" Johnny Dillard asked as he tugged on his suspenders.

"It was an old lady, and she looked just like my Great-grandma Cutler without her false teeth," Retta reported.

"You really traded that purple dress of yours for the buckskin?" Christen asked.

"It was pansy-plum-colored."

"Were you scared?" Gilson pressed.

"Nope."

Christen leaned her shoulder against Retta's. "Did you puff your cheeks out?"

"I guess."

"You were scared then."

The others nodded agreement.

"Well, maybe a little . . . at first."

Joslyn rubbed her hand along the beadwork on Retta's cuffs. "Can I wear your buckskin dress sometime?"

"Sure."

"We all want to wear that dress," Christen added.

"It's very comfortable," Retta admitted.

Ben Weaver pushed his way into the group gathered at the back of the Barres' covered wagon. "Retta, did you talk to them in sign language. Did they have bows and arrows or guns—or both? Did they have any scalps in their belts?"

Ben wants to talk to me now? He never wants to talk to me. She stared for a minute until Joslyn poked her in the ribs. "Oh, I didn't need to use sign language. Two Bears speaks English very well."

Ben stepped closer until he was only a foot away from Retta. He towered over her. "The man's name is Two Bears?"

Retta tried to step back, but Joslyn shoved her forward. "Yes, and his wife is named Lucy Two Bears. One son is Bear Heart. The daughter that I traded dresses with is Shy Bear."

"How old is Bear Heart?" Joslyn asked.

"He's younger than we are. He wasn't even as tall as his horse stick."

"His what?" Ben asked.

"Eh, it's a long story," Retta said.

"Can you tell it to me sometime?" Ben pressed.

Christen shoved her elbow into Retta's ribs and giggled.

"Sure," Retta said. Then she turned to Joslyn. "Two Bears does have older boys, but I didn't learn their names. Yet."

"Yet? You mean, you're going back?" Joslyn exclaimed.

Ansley MacGregor carried a pink parasol and tiptoed across the muddy trail. Everyone paused as she approached. "My father says it's very dangerous for you to go near Indians." She pushed her way past Ben Weaver.

Retta glanced around the group, who waited for her to speak. "These were not dangerous Indians."

"How do you know?" Ansley challenged.

"They were just a family. How dangerous can a mother with a baby and an old lady without teeth be?"

"Did you call them by their Indian names?" Johnny Dillard asked.

Sprinkles dripped off Ansley's parasol. Retta scooted away so they wouldn't mark her buckskin dress. "Yes. They even gave me an Indian name."

"Really?" Ben blurted out. "What is it? Is it really awful?"

"No, I like it. They said I have the same name they have."

"What do you mean?" Gilson asked.

"Both of us pronounce our last names 'Bear.' Two Bears thought my first name, Retta, sounded sort of like red. So he called me 'Red Bear.'"

"You don't have red hair. You can't be called 'Red.'" Ansley spun the parasol in her hand, showering those around her. "You have to have the characteristic before you can have the nickname. I simply won't share it with a brunette."

Gilson stared down at her black high-top, lace-up shoes. "You get mad if any of us call you 'Red,'" she murmured.

"Yes, that's my right, don't you see?" Ansley insisted.

Joslyn Jouppi spun her parasol, and water splashed across Ansley's face. "Your daddy is sometimes called 'Tiny,' and he weighs over three hundred pounds. A person doesn't always need the characteristic to be called something."

"That's quite different," Ansley huffed.

"Retta, are you going to visit them again?" Ben asked.

"If I can. They did invite me back."

"How can you go back?" Travis Lott pulled off his felt hat and slapped it against the back of the wagon. "The wagon train will be on down the trail."

"I believe we'll be stuck in the mud for a couple of days."

"Who says? It hasn't rained that much," Johnny challenged.

"You wait and see," Retta maintained.

"If you go to visit them Indians again, can I go?" Ben asked.

"I guess. But you can't take your gun."

"We all want to go!" Joslyn proclaimed.

"Well, I don't. I think that's terribly foolish," Ansley taunted.

"Maybe 'cause you're scared and Retta isn't," Joslyn offered.

Ansley's neck stiffened. "Posh. Ansley MacGregor is afraid of nothing."

"You were afraid of that scorpion the other day when your folks were busy with that sick ox. I had to come rescue you," Ben reminded her.

"Oh, when was this, Ansley? We didn't hear," Christen prodded.

"It was nothing," Ansley mumbled.

"That ain't what you said that day," Ben reported.

Lerryn Barre poked her head out of the back of the wagon. "Miss Pocahontas had better start helping mother with supper!"

"We better get back to our wagons. I think it's starting to rain harder," Christen observed.

"Two Bears said it would be a downpour," Retta informed her.

"Can I talk to you later about the Indians?" Ben asked her.

Joslyn poked Retta in the ribs. "Sure," Retta blurted out.

Thunder rolled across the dark low-hanging clouds. Retta felt the rain pelt her face.

"You can walk under my parasol!" Ansley called to Ben.

"I don't need no umbrella," he hollered as he jogged through the downpour. "I ain't goin' to melt."

Mr. Barre had pitched a white canvas awning next to their wagon. Retta squatted near the smoldering chip fire. Her mother gazed into the black cast-iron pot that hung from a hook.

"I don't know if we're goin' to have warm stew or cold," Mrs. Barre fumed.

Retta fanned the smoldering chips with a cedar shingle that had a picture of a horse on it. She had painted the picture. "Mama, did you know that in a Shoshone camp, the old women tend the fire?"

She watched as her mother repeatedly rubbed her temples with her fingertips.

"Do you feel okay, Mama?" she asked.

"I'm sick to my stomach. I can't believe your father let you wander off like that. If I told him once, I've told him a thousand times, 'Eugene Barre, don't you be dragging us off to Oregon and jeopardize the safety of my children.'"

"I guess we're Papa's children too, Mama," Retta murmured.

Mrs. Barre stood up straight and rubbed her hand slowly over her apron-covered stomach. "Sometimes he doesn't act like it."

"I didn't wander off, Mama. I was just warning the men to bring the cattle in like you asked me to."

"And I told you to go with someone."

"They were all busy or asleep. What was I supposed to do?"

Mrs. Barre stared off into the stormy clouds. One hand rested on the pole that suspended the white canvas awning. The other hand pressed against the small part of her back. "You were supposed to use discretion, young lady—not go traipsing off with wild Indians."

Retta scooted up next to her. "Mama, I prayed about it. Honest, I did."

Mrs. Barre stood about two inches taller than Retta. She put her arm around her daughter's shoulders. "You could have gotten into horrible trouble, Coretta Emily."

"But I didn't, Mama." Retta laced her fingers in her mother's. "The Lord looked after me."

Mrs. Barre squeezed her hand. "I don't think you should go to an Indian camp again. There's no reason to try God's patience."

"But they're my friends."

Mrs. Barre pulled a skinny loaf of bread from the large wooden box near the fire. She sliced it as if killing snakes.

"Nonsense. They are Indians. They are totally different from us."

"That's not completely true," Retta mumbled.

"What did you say?" Mrs. Barre snapped.

"Nothing, Mama." Retta stirred up the fire and retrieved another dry chip from under the wagon. *Lord, it surely seems to me that all families are sort of alike, aren't they? I mean, Jesus died for us all, so we must all be in about the same mess.* "Mama, when we left Independence, you said I should try to be more friendly. I was just trying to be friendly."

"I meant with your own kind."

"Who are my kind, Mama?"

"Coretta Emily, don't you sass your mama."

"I'm sorry, Mama. But Lerryn's kind is you, and William's and Andrew's kind is Papa. But how about me, Mama? Who are my kind?"

"You are one of a kind, Coretta Emily. There is no one just like you."

"Maybe I don't have a kind."

"Coretta!"

"I didn't mean for that to be mouthy. I'm just trying to understand."

Mrs. Barre put her hand on her forehead and let out a long sigh. "It's okay, darlin'. I know I'm jumpy. I can never seem to get rid of this headache. Sometimes I can't even see straight, let alone think straight. Did you see Andrew?"

"He's taking his turn on the perimeter."

"He seems young to stand guard."

"Mr. Bouchet says Andy is the best horse wrangler in the whole camp, not counting him and Colonel Graves."

"I suppose William went with your father. Not that anyone asked my permission."

"William's twenty, Mama. He sort of likes to make up his own mind. You know that."

Mrs. Barre stared across the prairie at the rainstorm. Retta saw her eyes narrow and jaw tighten. "I don't know why he had to go out there. It's getting dark and pouring rain."

"Really, Mama, they'll be fine. They just wanted to meet my friend Two Bears."

"Yes, and there was nothing I could do to stop your father. He should be here, and he knows it. What if there's trouble? What if the Indians show up here? What if I need him?"

Retta saw tears trickle down her mother's cheeks.

"It's all right, Mama. Papa can take care of himself, and I can take care of you."

"That's the job of Colonel Graves and Mr. Bouchet. I don't know why Eugene always has to ride off like that." The stew spoon began to quiver in her hand.

"Two Bears and his family are very nice and mean us no harm."

"Baby, there are other Indians out there. If good ones can camp that close without us knowing it, so can the mean ones. I don't know what we're doing out here. All I ever wanted was our little white house in Barresville. I don't know why I'm out here on this deserted prairie," Mrs. Barre sobbed.

Retta hugged her mother's waist. "It's okay, Mama. Papa will be fine. You wait and see."

"We're gone two months, and what do we have to show for it? We're stuck in this mud. I don't like the rain, baby. I just don't like the rain. I didn't like the rain in Ohio. I don't like the rain here. And I know I'm not going to like the rain in Oregon."

"We can trust the Lord."

Mrs. Barre hugged her daughter just as Lerryn scampered under the awning with a black parasol over her head. "Mama, Mrs. Wingate traded a cup of raisins for the sugar."

"Good. If we stay put long enough, I'll bake raisin bread."

"We're going to be here three days," Retta announced.

"Oh?"

"I heard that if the wagons get stuck, it will take three days to dry out the ground enough to drive out of here."

"Three days with nothing to do but sit around and gossip!" Mrs. Barre fumed.

"The whole wagon train is already talking about the Barre girl who escaped capture by the Indians," Lerryn reported.

"Capture? They didn't capture me. They just let me stand in their cave so I could get out of the rain," Retta corrected her.

"Don't worry about it." Lerryn waltzed around under the awning. "Most of them think it was me."

"You?"

"They kept stopping me to ask me when I was going to wear my new buckskin dress."

Retta twirled around next to the fire. "My dress is pretty, isn't it?"

"I wonder if I altered it a little if it would fit me?" Lerryn pondered.

Retta puffed out her cheeks. "It's my dress," she muttered.

"Coretta is right," Mrs. Barre said. "It's all right for a little girl to play in such a dress, but you're much too old. Besides, I don't want you both dressed like wild Indians."

"I'm not exactly a little girl," Retta protested.

"Look!" Lerryn shouted. "Here come Papa and William!"

The fire smoldered.

The rain pelted down.

The canvas wagon top and awning dripped.

The air cooled.

The thunder growled.

Lightning assailed the prairie.

And Retta Barre was the talk of the camp.

After supper Mr. Barre put on a dry shirt and left it unbuttoned as he sipped coffee by the fire. "Do you want some coffee?" he asked.

Retta took a sip from his tin cup. "You couldn't find any trace of the Indians?"

"Nope. The rain came up, and there were no tracks at all."

"Did you find the cave back in the riverbed?" she pressed.

"No. And we rode up and down the river half a dozen times."

"But it was there. I saw it. I was standing in it with Two Bears and his family."

"I believe you, darlin'. You're wearin' the proof."

"Do you like my dress, Papa?"

"Darlin', any dress you wore would look beautiful."

"I love you, Papa." She hugged him tight and laid her head on his hard, muscled bare chest.

"I love you too, darlin'." He ran his fingers through her thick, dark brown hair. "But Mama's right. No more explorin' the river by yourself. Mr. Bouchet said that the farther west we get, the more dangerous the Indians are."

"You mean, if someone goes with me, I could go see them again?"

"Perhaps. I'll talk to your mama about it. But I reckon that band you ran across moved out, 'cause we surely didn't find them."

"You want me to keep the fire going, Papa?"

"Is Mama lyin' down to rest?"

"Yes. She got very worried when you and William left. Her head was hurting again."

"You know how Mama is. She loves us all so much it scares her sometimes," he added as he buttoned his shirt.

"I know, Papa. I love us all, too."

"Keep the fire hot for Andrew. I'll go spell him off."

Retta squatted down next to the fire in the dark. The only light flickered from a lamp inside the covered wagon and the smoldering coals. William and Lerryn scooted off toward the lamps of other wagons.

This has been a very adventuresome day, Lord. Can a person have too much adventure? I believe this was just the right amount. I'm the only one who has met Indians. I wonder why that was? Did You want me to say something to them about You?

She had the dishes washed, dried, and packed in the crate when she heard a scuffling noise from under the covered wagon.

"Pssst . . . Red Bear!"

Retta leaped away from the wagon and looked under the canvas sling that held the chips. "Who's there?"

There was no answer.

"Is that you, Ben Weaver?"

She sauntered back to the wagon, squatted down, and whispered, "Ben Weaver, you shouldn't be here. If my mama finds out, she'll pitch a fit."

Still no answer.

"I know you're there, Ben. This isn't funny. Did Travis and Johnny put you up to this?" She reached her hand into the dark. "Now come on out before you get us both in trouble."

"I am not who you think I am, Red Bear."

A bare, dark-skinned arm reached out and latched onto her hand.

This time she recognized the voice.

"Two Bears?" Retta gasped.

Six

"Who is Benweaver?" The voice sounded like it was somewhere between a laugh and a growl.

Retta dropped to her knees and peeked under the wagon. "Two Bears, what are you doing here?" she whispered.

"Is Benweaver your boyfriend?"

"No!"

"Oh. Do lots of boys crawl under your wagon to peek at you?"

"No. I mean, Ben Weaver is my best friend's brother, and he has sort of a cute smile and—what are you doing here?"

Even in the dark his white teeth shone. "Visiting my relative, Red Bear."

"How did you get here without anyone seeing you?"

"I simply went where they didn't look for me. I have a question. Why were the white men looking for me?"

"I think they just wanted to visit, to make sure you weren't going to attack the wagon train."

"Attack the wagon train with two boys and some women and a baby?"

"I told them not to worry, but I don't think they believed me."

"Why don't they believe you, Red Bear? Do you lie often?"

"No. But I'm just a girl."

"They don't believe girls?"

"Sometimes they don't," Retta admitted. "Anyway, everyone is kind of afraid of Indians. They didn't find your cave."

"Of course not. Should I be afraid of them?"

"No. My papa isn't scary, and neither is my brother William."

"Who is the gray-bearded man?"

"Mr. Bouchet. He's our scout."

"He looks familiar."

"You saw him?"

"They came within a few feet of where I stood."

"And they didn't see you?"

"Of course not."

A deep male voice echoed out of the dark, and she stood straight up. "Li'l sis, you got a lamp?"

She waited for him to come within view. "Hi, Andrew."

He reached into the back of the wagon and pulled out the lamp. "Who were you talkin' to, Retta?"

"Oh, you know how I am."

He laughed. "I know, you're always pretendin'."

"Sometimes that's the only way to have an adventure. Andrew, I've kept the stew warm for you."

"It looks like Mama's sleeping sound," he said, pointing to the dark wagon.

"You know how she is after she's worried all day."

He set the lamp on the ground. It cast light back under the wagon. Retta picked it up and slipped the handle over an iron hook up on the side of the wagon. "It's kind of muddy. We might kick the lamp over," she explained.

"Where's William?"

"He said he was going to visit with the colonel, but in this rain I bet he's at the Lynch wagon."

"And Lerryn?"

"Guess."

"At the Suetters'?"

"Yes."

"So it's just you and Mama?" Andrew asked.

Retta glanced back at the darkness under the box of the wagon. "Yes, but we're okay. Where do you need to go?"

"Nowhere." Andrew scooped up a big spoonful of stew and stuffed it in his mouth. "I'm goin' to sit right here by the fire and eat supper and slurp coffee until I've dried out."

"Right here?"

"I'm surely not goin' to wake up Mama in the wagon. I'll keep you company."

"I don't need company. What I mean is, I'm okay by myself. Just me and Mama."

"No, li'l sis, I ain't goin' nowhere," Andrew insisted.

"Never?"

He stared at her.

Retta swallowed hard. "You're in for the evening?"

"Yep. I turned Beanie out with the other horses. I've already done my shift. So unless there's a stampede, I'm through for the night."

"Well, eh . . . maybe," Retta began as she danced on one foot and then the other, "since you're here and all, maybe I'll go for a little walk myself."

"It's all right under this awning, but you don't want to go out in the rain."

"I'll take a parasol."

"It's pitch-dark."

"I'm not afraid of the dark," she proclaimed.

"Don't you go runnin' off. I need you here with Mama."

"Why? You'll be here."

Andrew sipped coffee out of a tin cup. "'Cause I just might think of somewhere I need to go after a while."

Retta shot a glance into the dark shadows under the wagon, but she could not see anything. *This is the only evening in the last two weeks that Andrew isn't going down the wagon line visiting! Poor Two Bears.*

"Hey, did you guys see him?" a voice shouted in the darkness.

Andrew stepped to the edge of the awning but kept out of the rain. "It's William! See who?" he called out.

Retta's oldest brother hiked in dripping wet and scrunched down by the fire. Water rolled off his floppy-brimmed felt hat. "He came right through camp."

"He did?" she gulped.

William pulled off his wire-framed spectacles and searched for a dry place on his bandanna. "Headin' right this way, they say."

"Oh, my!" she gasped.

Andrew reached for the coffeepot. "Who are you talkin' about?"

"Did either of you see ol' Mr. Skunk?"

"A skunk?" Retta laughed. "That's what this conversation is about?"

"That's what I've been sayin'." William shoved his spectacles back on his nose and held his hands over the coals of the fire.

"No, I don't think I've seen a skunk up close since we left Missouri," Retta remarked.

"Maybe he's under our wagon." Andrew pointed.

"No," Retta blurted out. "I mean, I would have seen it if it were under our wagon!"

Andrew plucked the lantern off the iron hook. "Remember the time Retta tried to keep that raccoon in her room back home?"

William hooted. "He shredded the curtains and the quilt and made regular deposits in her dresser drawer."

Retta puffed out her cheeks and rocked back on her heels. "It wouldn't have torn the quilt if Lerryn hadn't chased it with a broom," she exploded.

Andrew bent low with the lamp.

Retta bit her lip. *Please, Lord! Help Two Bears not to get hurt.*

"Nope, nothin' under here," Andrew reported. "But I can almost smell that skunk. I bet he went right through here."

Retta pulled a bucket next to the wagon and flopped down. Andrew and William squatted by the fire.

"You want to come over here, Retta?" William asked.

"I'm kind of tired. I think I'll stay here, thank you."

"If you want to crawl into the wagon and go to sleep, we'll keep the fire goin'," William said.

"I can't go to sleep until Lerryn comes back. You know how she flounces around getting ready for bed."

"Maybe we should go fetch her," William offered.

Retta brushed her damp bangs off her eyes. "Eh . . . maybe so."

"I'm not in a hurry to rile big sis," Andrew protested. "Let's just wait awhile."

"This rain surely came up in a hurry. They say Oregon gets a lot of rain," William remarked.

"And the crops grow tall," Andrew replied.

"And the winters are mild."

"And the soil don't have any rocks."

"And there is plenty of water and grass."

"Do you really believe all of that?" Andrew asked.

"I don't," William said. "But Papa does, and that's all that matters."

"Mama is still melancholy over leaving Ohio," Retta informed them.

William stirred up the fire with a stick. "I think it's rough to go off and leave everyone behind."

"Especially in her condition and all," Andrew said.

"Uncle Lambert claimed they might move out to Oregon next year. If he moved out, she wouldn't be so lonesome." Andrew filled his bowl with more stew.

"I thought he said he wanted to move to California," Retta said.

"Well, one or the other. Even California would be a little closer."

Retta peered into the shadows under the wagon. She still could not see Two Bears.

He must have slipped off. That's good. It was dangerous for him to be this close. He could get shot. Lord, I never thought when this day began that I'd be praying for an Indian. I guess You knew that. It's like You and me, Lord, are the only ones who know Two Bears came to camp.

I hope!

William poured his coffee cup full. "Sis, I'm proud of you dealing with the Indians today, no matter what anyone else says."

Retta stood and strolled over to her brothers. "What do you mean, anyone else? What are they saying?"

"Oh, you know how people are."

"William Henry Barre, what did they say?"

"Some are sayin' that you cheated the Indians out of that buckskin dress, and when they figure that out, they might show up and cause a ruckus."

"Cheated?" Retta gasped. "Shy Bear begged me to trade!"

William gulped down his coffee. "I didn't say it was true, Retta. I just said that's what some people say."

"What people?" she pressed.

Andrew tossed down his stew bowl. "You know . . . people."

"What people, Andrew?"

"Like Ansley MacGregor, for one," he replied.

"Ansley? She's just jealous because she doesn't have a buckskin dress."

Andrew wiped his mouth on his gray cotton shirtsleeve. "You might be right there."

"But Colonel Graves did say it would be best to let him and Mr. Bouchet make all the contacts with Indians," William added.

"I didn't really have any choice. The boy was hurt. What was I supposed to do?"

"You did the right thing, li'l sis. We're on your side," William assured her.

Andrew let the hot coffee steam his face. "I won't even tell you what Mr. MacGregor said."

"He talked about me?" Retta asked.

"He said that you runnin' around on the prairie without a bonnet, getting tanned and all, made you look like an Indian."

"What was his purpose in saying that?" William fumed.

"Maybe that's something you and me ought to ask him."

"Right now?" Retta asked.

"Ain't doin' nothin' in this rain." Andrew pulled off his hat and ran his fingers through his light brown hair. "Retta, what did that Indian of yours look like?"

Retta glanced under the wagon. "He was shorter than you two, very lean but with muscles, black hair down to his shoulders, clean-shaven. Do Indians shave?"

William shrugged "I don't think so."

Retta looked under the wagon again. "Brown eyes, brown skin, kind of round face, but a pointed chin and a scar. He had very white, straight teeth and a nice smile that he didn't use much."

"Sounds like you really studied him. Some would have been too scared to remember."

"It wasn't that long ago." She fought the urge to peek back under the wagon. "Besides, I was with them for quite a while during the storm."

"I hear Indian girls can be quite fetching," Andrew said. "Did you see any . . . you know . . ."

Retta giggled. "Quite-fetching Indian girls?"

"Yeah." Andrew's narrow gray eyes danced in the glow of the fire.

Retta bit her lip. "The oldest girl was the one who traded me dresses. She was quite pretty. Had beautiful waist-length hair."

"And she fits in your old purple dress?" Andrew asked.

"The color of my dress was pansy plum. And it wasn't all that old. Mama made it for me for Christmas."

Andrew laughed. "Anyone who fits in that dress is not 'quite fetching.'"

Retta stared down at her shoes. *I fit in that dress; so I reckon I know what you think I look like.*

William jammed his hat back on. "Did they say anything about whether more Indians are around?"

"No, but I didn't ask. He's a Shoshone."

"We're not in Shoshone country," William remarked.

"He and his family are on their way home to Fort Bridger."

"Are they fixin' to parallel us?" Andrew quizzed.

"I don't know, but he did say they kept a close eye on our wagon train."

"They're watching us? Why?" Andrew asked.

"I think they're worried about what we might do."

"About what *we* will do? How about them?" William declared.

"They're not a dangerous group. But they did know that I was in the wagon with the yellow flap at the back."

Andrew's neck and shoulders stiffened. "I can't believe they knew that."

"Well, they did."

William stared into the darkness toward the river. "They could be watching us right now."

Retta glanced back at the wagon and puffed her cheeks out. "Could be they can see us sittin' right here."

William turned back to the fire. "Don't go around tellin' others that. Ever'one will be imagining Indians ever'where."

"Don't you think it's time you went to fetch Lerryn?" Retta suggested.

"Andrew can do that," William replied. "I don't need to go."

"I thought you both wanted to go."

"No need for that," William said.

"I'm not goin' to face sis's wrath by myself," Andrew said. "She'll be madder than Mrs. Gorman when she won second place at the pie-making contest at the county fair."

"Remember that time she tossed her pie at the judge? It was the best fair ever," William hooted. "But you might be right. We'll both go fetch her."

"I'll keep the fire going," Retta said.

She watched as her brothers pulled down their wide-brimmed felt hats and scurried out into the rain. She scooted over to the wagon and squatted down next to the canvas sling stretched between the two axles.

"Two Bears? Are you still there?" she whispered.

"Yes, Red Bear, I am here."

"Where are you?"

"With the buffalo droppings."

"In the chip sling?"

"Yes, it is quite cozy." He peeked out from the piles of dried buffalo dung.

"Why didn't you slip away?"

"I wanted to talk to you."

"What about?"

"I want to make another trade," he whispered.

"Do you want the buckskin dress back?"

He rolled out of the chip sling but remained under the wagon. "Oh, no, I want a book."

"A book? Did you say you wanted a book?"

"Yes."

"What book?"

"Any book will do. When I was scout for Jim Bridger, they taught me to read."

"Mr. Bridger taught you to read?" she queried.

"No, he does not know how himself. Mr. Sublette taught me. But I have no book to practice with. I want to teach my children to read also."

Retta rubbed her neck and could feel dirt roll under her fingertips. "So you want any old book?"

"Yes, as long as it has many words."

"And what do you want to trade for it?" Retta asked.

"Moccasins."

"Really?"

"They go with the dress, but they are old."

"Oh, yes! I would very much like to have some moccasins."

"Come to our cave tomorrow," Two Bears instructed.

"But how can I find it? The men couldn't find it."

"You will find it. You are family. Just come."

"Can I bring some friends with me?"

"As long as there is no gun. My children are afraid of men with guns."

"Okay, no guns."

"Good. Now I will go. Or perhaps I should just sleep with the droppings. It is very comfortable and warm."

"You'd better go before men with guns find you here."

"You are right. Good night, Red Bear."

"Good night, Two Bears."

He slipped out from under the wagon and disappeared into the dark night to the south of the wagon train. Retta built up the fire and poked at the coals. Then she washed Andrew's stew dish.

Sometimes, Lord, it's like I'm in a dream. I can't see Two Bears, but I'm talking to him. He's nothing like the stories I've read and heard. I wonder why that is? Perhaps Two Bears is the nicest Indian on the plains. If so, thank You for letting me meet him. Now I must find a way to give him a book.

"Coretta Emily!"

Retta sat straight up. "Yes, Mama?" *I thought she was asleep.*

"Will you come up here in the wagon for a minute?"

Retta ran over to the front of the wagon and climbed up in the wagon seat. She stuck her head inside the canvas flap. "Are you feeling better, Mama?"

Her mother was propped up on quilts and pillows at the far end of the wagon. She rubbed her stomach and then stretched her arms. "Yes, thank you. Did your father go out to patrol?"

"Yes."

"Have your brothers come in?"

"Yes. They just went to fetch Lerryn. What can I do for you, Mama?"

"Give him the extra copy of *Pilgrim's Progress*."

"What?" Retta gasped.

"We have two copies of Bunyan's book. Many a child has learned to read from it. Trade your Indian friend, Mr. Two Bears, a copy of *Pilgrim's Progress* for the moccasins. Perhaps they will learn to trust the Lord by reading it."

Retta puffed out her cheeks. "Did you hear us talking?"

"Yes, of course."

Retta crawled all the way into the wagon. "And you aren't mad at me?"

"No, I listened to his voice. He *is* a nice man."

"You can tell that by a man's voice?"

"Yes, I can. Young lady, a lot can be learned by listening to a man."

"How about boys? Can you learn something about boys by listening to them?"

"With boys," Mrs. Barre said smiling, "you must watch their eyes."

"Are you goin' to tell Papa and the others that Two Bears came to camp to see me?"

"Not unless he asks. How about you? Are you going to tell him?"

"Not unless he asks," Retta murmured.

Seven

Retta woke up with cold feet, damp blankets, and an elbow in her ribs. She pulled on her buckskin dress quickly and left her sister asleep in the wagon.

"Mornin', Mama," she said as she climbed down out of the wagon. "It surely did rain a lot last night."

"Good morning, young lady. And it's nice not to be awakened by a gunshot at 4:00 A.M."

"I reckon that's the good thing about being stuck in the mud."

"How about pulling on your shoes and building up the fire?" Mrs. Barre loosened her apron and kneaded the small of her back.

Retta rubbed her eyes and then perched on an upside-down milk bucket to tug on her stockings and shoes. "I wish I had those moccasins this morning," she said.

Mrs. Barre retied the apron and rubbed her temples with her fingertips. "You might have a chance to do some trading after all. Colonel Graves said it could be up to three days before we can move the wagons. All that dust in those wagon ruts has turned to mud and slime."

Retta stood and wiggled her toes in the nearly clean socks. "Three days is a long delay. Papa said we were already behind schedule."

"It's been rainier than expected," Mrs. Barre replied. "I hear we might stay at Fort Laramie only one night now."

"But—but you need to stay where there's a doctor and . . ."

"Not everything goes according to our plans. It's the Lord's plans that matter most. And He's in charge of the weather . . . and the Barre family."

Retta pulled out several dry chips from under the wagon and stoked the smoky fire. "William said there are some wagons that are way too heavy. Did you know Mrs. Norman has a pump organ in hers?"

"Yes, and I heard rumbling by some that are in a hurry."

"Who's complaining, Mama?" Retta fanned the fire with the painted shingle.

"The California-bound rigs, the single men on horseback, and those in lighter wagons. They are talking about going on ahead of us on their own."

"But we're supposed to stay together until we get past Fort Hall," Retta declared. She stared down into the three-legged skillet. "Are those potato cakes?"

"Yes. Don't they look like it?"

"But they have the peelings still on them."

"They're good for you."

"You always peel the potatoes."

"Well, I didn't this morning."

"Are you sick again, Mama?"

"Baby, you know me—I always feel a little puny early. I get stronger as the day goes on. Anyway, some in the train are mighty impatient. I'm not sure they will wait three days."

Retta slipped her fingers into her mother's strong, callused, pale hand. In comparison, Retta's fingers looked short, plump, and brown. "I hope they don't go. I like all the people in our wagon train. . . . Well, almost all of them."

"Some are talking like they might leave tomorrow."

"It will be too muddy."

"Maybe it's all just talk. They are frustrated, no doubt." Mrs. Barre put her hand on Retta's shoulder. "Now, young lady, I want to apologize for sounding so frightened and discouraged yesterday. I don't know what gets into me sometimes."

"It's okay, Mama. Everybody gets discouraged sometimes."

"Yes, well, I hope your papa can bring some encouragement to those who want to leave. The safest thing for all of us is to stick close together. They say that between here and Fort Hall there could be Indian trouble."

Retta stared down the endless row of wagons, each harboring a hurried blur of activity. "Did Papa go to talk to the California-bound?"

"He and Colonel Graves called a meeting."

The sun broke across the prairie and began to rise into a cloudless pale blue sky. Steam swirled off the canvas wagon tops, awnings, and tents. Retta turned toward the river. *Lord, Joslyn is going to California. I would really miss her. Maybe You can find a way to keep them with us.*

She stared at the canvas sling under the wagon. "Mama, what do we do when we run out of buffalo chips? The ones out there are all mushy and won't burn."

"I suppose we will eat cold meals."

"Cold potatoes?" Retta moaned. "I could get sick on cold potatoes."

Mrs. Barre grabbed the three-legged skillet and balanced it over the dug-out fire pit. "Mrs. O'Day said Gilson was worse today," she reported. "I don't think she'll be able to gather chips for a while."

"I wish she wasn't sick all the time. I pray and pray for her. Do you think the Lord hears my prayers?"

"Yes, I do. Just think how sick she might be if you didn't pray."

Retta dusted a few flakes of buffalo chip from her buckskin skirt. "May I go see her?"

Mrs. Barre waved toward the covered wagon. "After you wake sis up for me. Even if we aren't on the trail, she needs to milk the cows."

"Me? Wake her up?"

One glare sent Retta to the wagon. The flap was still damp from the rain. She crawled over the seat and into the wagon bed. The quilts were wadded in the corner near Great-grandma Cutler's brass clock and the crate of dishes. Lerryn was flopped on top of the covers, her head sunk deep in her feather pillow.

Retta studied her sister.

Lord, Lerryn is so pretty, so perfect. She must be the prettiest girl in the whole world. I'm happy You made her that way, but sometimes I sort of wish You would have saved a little bit for me. Not that I'm complaining, but everyone who knows her and then meets me says, "YOU are Lerryn's sister?" I wouldn't have to be fancy-pretty like her, if only I was sort of pretty . . . like Christen . . . or cute-pretty like Joslyn . . . or even pale-pretty like Gilson. Papa thinks I'm cute, but everyone knows that papas are very silly when it comes to their daughters.

Sometimes I wish someone would say, "Oh, you must be Lerryn's sister. I noticed the family resemblance." Lord, I don't look like anyone. Papa says we're created in Your image, so maybe I resemble You . . . sort of.

Retta pulled a small hand mirror from a green valise and scooted closer to Lerryn. She stared at the mirror and then peered at her sister.

Do You see what I mean, Lord? Look at her eyes, her eyebrows, those long eyelashes. Look at her nose—it's small and dainty. And mine? It looks like someone stuck a little round hunk of clay on my face. Look at my hair. There are horse manes that are prettier than this. Lerryn has very pretty lips. I heard Brian Suetter tell her once that she had very kissable lips.

Retta scooted down until her head was only a few inches from her sister's. She studied her own lips in the mirror. *My lips are puffy-looking, like I was stung by a bee. And they're kind of chapped and dark, not pale. I don't think I have kissable lips.*

Retta puckered up her lips and studied them in the mirror. *Is this what a kiss looks like close up? Kind of like a carp? No wonder Lerryn closes her eyes when she kisses Brian. It must feel better than it looks.*

She held her lips in an exaggerated pucker and pulled the mirror closer. She closed her eyes and pressed her lips against the mirror. It felt cold and slick and hard. *Well, it better be a whole lot more fun than this, or it's a waste of time.*

"What are you doing!" Lerryn shouted.

Retta dropped the mirror on the quilts and jumped to her feet.

Her sister sat straight up, waved her hands in the air, and screamed, "Get out of here!"

Retta scampered out of the wagon onto the wooden seat.

"What's going on in there?" Mrs. Barre asked.

Retta jumped down off the wagon. "I just woke her up like you asked me to," she mumbled.

"What was all the screaming about?"

"I guess we startled each other."

"Mother!" Lerryn yelled.

"Can I go see how Gilson is?" Retta asked.

"Mother, I need to talk to you!" Lerryn hollered.

"Just a minute, Lerryn. Yes, go on, Retta, but don't stay long. I'll have breakfast ready soon."

Retta raced down the row of wagons.

A tall, thin woman fried meat in an iron spider skillet over a small fire. Their campsite was littered with wooden cases and dining room chairs.

"Good mornin', Mrs. O'Day."

The woman wiped flour off her hands. "Hello, Retta dear. What was all that screaming in your wagon?"

"Lerryn saw something that frightened her when she first woke up," Retta replied.

"A scorpion or a snake?"

"Whatever it was must have been very scary. May I check on Gilson?"

"Please do. Perhaps you can talk her into eating some biscuits and gravy."

Retta crawled up on the O'Day wagon and stuck her head inside the flap. Gilson had a dark green comforter pulled up to her chin. Her thin blonde hair stuck out in several directions.

"Good mornin', yellow-haired girl," Retta called out.

First one eye, then the other opened. Gilson didn't move anything else. "Hi, Retta."

Retta scooted in next to her friend and sat on an ox-hide-covered trunk. "I heard you're feeling poorly today."

Gilson pulled the comforter down to her shoulders. "Do you ever think about dying, Retta?"

Retta's hand went to her mouth. "I try not to."

Gilson raised up on one elbow and leaned closer. "Why? Why don't you want to think about dying? It's as natural as eating and breathing, isn't it?"

Retta brushed the girl's blonde bangs back out of her eyes. "What kind of talk is this? I come here to cheer up my sick friend, and you want to talk about dying?"

Gilson laid her head back down and closed her eyes. "Sometimes I think about it," she murmured.

"Remember two weeks ago when I ate those berries that I thought were ripe, but they weren't, and I got sick to my stomach?" Retta asked.

"Yes."

"I sort of wanted to die that day."

"I want to die every day."

Retta rocked back and forth. *Lord, this talk is scaring me. I don't know what to say.* "What are you talking about?"

Tears trickled out of Gilson's eyes and plunged to the pillow. "I'm so sick and tired of being sick and tired all the time, Retta."

"I don't want you talking about dying. You aren't going to die for a long, long time. We're moving out West, and it is very, very healthy out there. We are going to live to be old ladies with dozens of grandchildren, and we'll sit around in the church basement making quilts and making up stories about the Oregon Trail."

"Making up stories?"

"Well, there hasn't been very much excitement on our journey. Besides, when you're ninety years old, you can't remember anything. So we'll have to make up things," Retta declared. "Maybe we should practice."

Gilson opened both eyes again. "What do you mean?"

Retta reached down and took her hand. "Why don't you sit up, and we'll pretend we are old and quilting."

"Really?"

"Sure, I'll help you." Retta pulled Gilson to a sitting position and then sat down on the floor and spread the quilt out between them.

Retta pretended to have a needle in her hand. She held the quilt up as if sewing. "Well, honey, this quilt reminds me of one day when we were out on the trail. Do you remember that day?"

"Huh?"

"I'm pretending, Gilson. Pretend that we are very old and in Oregon and remembering this trip."

A slight smile crossed the blonde girl's pale face. "Oh, okay. Eh . . . which particular day were you thinking of, sweetie?"

"See . . . you can do it!" Retta called out. "Do you remember that day when the red-headed girl fell off that fancy black horse of hers and landed right in the fresh buffalo dung?"

Gilson giggled. "You mean, the MacGregor girl, dearie?"

"Was that her name? I can't remember."

"I think her first name was Ansley," Gilson said.

"Was that it, snookie? I thought her name was Pansy."

Both girls rolled over on the quilt in laughter.

Gilson coughed twice and gulped a big breath. "No, I'm sure it was Ansley. What do you suppose ever happened to her?"

"Didn't you hear?" Retta sat up, waving her hands in front of her.

"Hear what, dear one? Speak a little louder. That's my bad ear."

Retta shouted, "She never married!"

Gilson flashed a pretend look of shock. "No!"

"Yes, it's true. She's living in a small home in Baltimore with her mother."

"Her mother? Ansley must be ninety-one years old. Her mother would be 120!"

"Mother?" Retta laughed. "No, you misunderstood. I said her *brother*."

Gilson shook her head. "Ansley didn't have a brother. She was an only child."

"Oh, no. Don't you remember? He was born right after Fort Hall. Ansley was . . . eh . . . thirteen."

"Oh, yes, that brother!" Gilson clapped. "Well, it's a shame she never married. I wonder why that was?"

"No one ever asked her, I suppose."

"Yes, I reckon you're right."

Retta pretended to be sewing the quilt. "Do you remember how the boys used to follow after us on the trail?"

Gilson's entire body was rocking back and forth. "Oh, yes. It was quite embarrassing at times."

"You know, there were nights on the trail when I longed to be plain and simple like Ansley so that the boys would leave me alone." Retta raised her round nose and tried not to grin.

"Yes, I know what you mean, honey." Gilson glided her pretend needle along the quilt. "Although I suppose there are a few advantages in not being married or having children."

"Oh?"

"Think of all the washing and ironing she didn't have to do."

Retta nodded. "I see your point. And she certainly didn't have to go through childbirth six times like we did."

"Twelve times, dear," Gilson corrected.

"Twelve times?" Retta gasped.

"We both have twelve children. Remember?"

"Oh yes! Six boys and six girls."

Gilson's blue eyes flashed. "All this make-believe is getting painful."

"Well now, dearie, just remember, before you have babies, you have to have a husband that loves you and . . . you have to . . ." Retta slapped her hand over her mouth and giggled.

Gilson started to laugh. "Retta Emily Barre, are you being naughty?"

"Almost. Come on, get dressed. Let's go see if Ansley has fallen into the buffalo dung yet."

Gilson struggled to her feet. "Okay. Hand me my yellow dress. Not all of us have buckskin to wear."

Eight

The sun hung halfway down the western sky as Retta hiked along the line of wagons. She stopped at a large loaded Conestoga, the second biggest wagon in the train. "Hi, Ben, is Christen here?"

"Nah. She and Mom went up the line to see the Randolphs' new baby," the fourteen-year-old replied.

"A new baby? When was it born?"

"Last night, so I hear. What have you been doin' all day, Retta? You didn't go see your Indians, did you?"

Retta stared down at her shoes. "Papa wouldn't let me. He said it was too muddy. So me and Mama washed some clothes and ironed them. Mama ironed them. I just kept the fire and the irons hot."

"Iron clothes? She worries about that out here on the plains? My mama said she was not heatin' an iron until she gets to Oregon," Ben declared.

"You know how Mama is. She's very particular. 'Isolation is no excuse for being slovenly.' She was upset 'cause she didn't have any starch for her apron. What have you been doin', Ben?"

He jammed his floppy brown felt hat back on his head. "Mainly just listenin'. Some folks are giving the colonel a bad time. They want to break off and go on their own."

"I don't know why anyone would be in that big a hurry."

"Some think they are still goin' to find gold in California if they get there quick enough. They claim it would be better to leave tomorrow, even if we only go a few miles." Ben yanked his hunting knife from its sheath and bent over to scrape mud from his boots.

"When Papa signed onto the wagon train, he had to agree to do what the colonel says," Retta declared.

Ben scraped his other boot clean. "So did all the rest. But I reckon now they are changin' their minds."

"If we pull out tomorrow, I won't be able to go see Two Bears and his family," Retta said.

"Do you really think you can find them again?"

"Yes. I'll find them, or they'll find me."

"And you're going to take me with you, right?"

"Yes, but we have to include others, too."

Ben looked around as if expecting someone to be listening. "Why?"

Retta puffed out her cheeks. "It wouldn't look right!"

"What do you mean, it wouldn't look right? What are you talkin' about?"

"You're not so ignorant, Ben Weaver. You know perfectly well what I mean. A boy and a girl goin' off together to the river wouldn't be proper."

"You and me?" he hooted. "No one would say anything. You're only twelve years old."

"I'm twelve and a half. Besides, you just turned fourteen."

"I'm big for my age."

Retta glanced down at her buckskin dress. "And I am . . . I am . . . twelve and a half," she repeated.

"We've known each other all our lives. You—you're like a sister to me!" he exclaimed.

"I am not your sister, Ben Weaver," she snapped.

"I didn't mean that." He blushed. He shoved his knife back into the sheath. "Who do you want to take with us?"

"Christen and Joslyn and maybe Gilson, if she feels like it," Retta replied.

Ben pulled off his hat. His curly hair exploded like a jack-in-the-box. "You mean I have to go find the Indians with a bunch of girls?"

Retta crossed her arms across her chest. "No, you don't have to go at all, Benjamin Weaver! Besides, you were willing to go if it were only me."

"Yeah, but that's different." His smile revealed two dimples besides the one in his chin. "I want to see some Indians."

"We'll see them all right."

"But, you know, I was hopin' it would be just you and me."

Retta studied his eyes. "Why?"

"'Cause."

"Ben Weaver, what were you scheming?"

He dropped his smile and swallowed hard. "I just thought if I got really scared or something, no one would see me except you."

"And I don't count?" Retta asked.

"No!" He stared right back in her eyes. "Retta, you're always on my side. You and me have been pals for a long time. I know I could depend on you to help me and not tell anyone."

"I already promised the girls they could come," she explained. "But there won't be anything to be scared of with Two Bears."

"I don't think Joslyn will come with us tomorrow. I heard they were one of the wagons breakin' off the trail and goin' on."

Retta laced her fingers and pulled them to her lips. "No, they can't do that."

Ben pointed up the wagon row. "They have that light buckboard wagon and tent. Mr. Landers thinks they can make it with some of the men on horseback."

"But—but . . ." Retta held her breath, puffed out her cheeks, and then blurted out, "I don't want her to go."

"Maybe they won't do it," Ben murmured.

"I'm going to talk to Joslyn."

Ben grabbed her arm. "And you won't go see the Indians without me?"

Retta glanced at his hand and raised her eyebrows. "Nope."

Ben dropped his arm to his side. "And you won't tell anyone I was sort of afraid to go see them?"

"Nope," she said.

The wide dimple returned to his chin. "I knew I could count on you!"

Retta curled her lip down. "Yep, that's me—your pal." She hiked out from under the canvas awning.

Ben scurried up to her. "Wait a minute. I'll walk with you."

A wide grin draped her face as she walked alongside him. *Lord, I like it when Ben walks with me. It's not bad to like having a boy walk with you, is it?* "So you want to go see Joslyn with me?"

"Nah," he shrugged. "Ansley had somethin' she wanted to show me. So I have to walk up the line anyway."

Joslyn Jouppi stood in the soft mud about twenty feet from the wagon train. She stared west at the tall prairie grass. Her arms were folded across her chest, her back toward the wagons.

Retta tiptoed across the mud. "Joslyn?"

The girl didn't turn around. "Don't you come near me!"

"It's me—Retta."

"I know who it is. Don't come any closer."

"Why? What's wrong?"

"I don't want you to see me."

"But why?"

"Go away."

Retta sucked in her breath and puffed out her cheeks. Then she took another step. "But I want to see you!"

"We're leavin' the train, Retta."

"When?"

Joslyn's voice softened. "Tomorrow mornin' at daybreak."

"But . . . I don't want you to go, Joslyn." Retta took a couple more steps in the girl's direction.

"We're goin' to press on to California and become very, very rich."

"I like you whether you're rich or not."

Joslyn sniffled. "You aren't making this very easy."

Retta inched closer. "And you aren't even looking at me."

"I'm afraid to."

"Why?"

"'Cause I'll cry and cry."

"That's okay, Joslyn. Everyone needs to cry sometimes." Retta found a halfway dry place in the prairie dirt and kept moving forward.

"Not me. I've cried enough."

"What are you talking about?"

"Never mind. Go on."

Retta was now only a few feet behind the girl. "Are you chasing me off?"

"Yes."

"Well, I'm not going."

Joslyn spun around and took a step toward Retta. "I don't need any friends."

Retta stepped right up next to her. "Well, I do."

Joslyn threw her arms around Retta's shoulders and sobbed. "Go away. I don't want to cry!"

Retta hugged her back. "I'm not going away. You know that."

"Yeah, I was sort of counting on that. What am I goin' to do, Retta? What am I goin' to do? I hurt so bad on the inside I think I'll die."

"You have to go where your mama and papa want you to go."

"He's not my papa."

"You know what I mean."

"Retta, how come nobody ever asks me what I want to do?"

"What do you want to do?"

"Never to have to say good-bye to my friends."

"But when we get settled in Oregon and you in California, we can write and visit, just like we've always said."

"But we were going to have another month on the trail to be together before we split off."

"Maybe your papa will change his mind."

"Mr. Landers never changes his mind."

"Well . . . well . . ." Retta curled her lower lip. "It's not until tomorrow; so let's make sure we enjoy today," she finally said.

Joslyn hugged her tight. "Today's almost gone."

"We've got a few more hours before dark. Let's do something fun."

"What?"

"You name it. What would you like to do?"

"You mean, besides steal Ansley's horse and ride off into the sunset?"

"Yes," Retta giggled. "What else?"

"I want to go see your Indian friends."

"Now?"

"You said we still have time."

"But Papa said it was too muddy to leave the wagon train."

"Ask him again . . . please, Retta."

"I'll ask him. But if we can't, let's see if you can sleep in our wagon tonight!"

"Do you have room?"

"Andrew and William like to sleep outside. I'll go find Papa."

"Retta, I'm really, really goin' to miss you."

"You haven't gone yet. Maybe the Lord has a miracle in store."

"Not for me."

"Well, you can have one of my miracles."

"You'd give me one of yours?"

"Sure."

"I like that!" Joslyn smiled for the first time.

"I'll come back after I see Papa."

Every wagon in the line had blankets and sheets hanging outside drying from the night's downpour. The heels of Retta's shoes mashed down into the mud, which clung to her soles with each heavy step. Two dozen men hunkered at a campfire built under the awning of the second wagon. Retta spied William at the edge of the group, clutching the reins of two horses.

"Is Mama okay?" he asked.

"She's fine, I think. I just wanted to talk to Papa."

Her big brother pushed his spectacles up on the bridge of his nose. "He's busy over there."

"What are they talking about?" she asked.

"The California people want to pull out now."

"Do all of them want to leave?"

"Yep."

"But we were supposed to stay together until after Fort Hall."

"Yeah, well . . . I suppose they're gettin' gold fever. Word is that the wagon train behind us is out on the trail today."

"Maybe it didn't rain so hard back there."

"Yeah, that's what Papa is tellin' them."

"I thought it was too muddy for the big wagons."

"They are talkin' about pulling out at daylight, letting their cattle and horses stamp down the trail, and see if the wagons can follow."

"Why don't we all do that?"

"The colonel says that even if it works, it will make the trail so rutted that it would be almost unusable for those who follow."

"What's Papa telling them?"

"That we if cut short a stay at Fort Laramie, we can still get to Fort Hall by August 1, and that's what we were aimin' at. He said the women and children would be safer in the bigger train."

Retta stood on her tiptoes and tried to peek through the crowd. "I really need to talk to Papa."

"Don't interrupt him now, Retta."

"When he's done, will you tell him I need to talk to him really, really bad?"

William leaned closer. "Are you in trouble again?"

"Again? I'm not in trouble. I just want to ask his permission for something."

"Oh?"

"Tell him I need to talk to him."

"He might be here a long time, but I'll tell him. I like your dress, li'l sis."

She twirled around. "Isn't it nice? It will look even better when I get my moccasins."

"You're getting moccasins?"

"Someday I hope to."

Christen waited for her at the Weaver wagon. "Did you see the new baby?"

"No. Is he cute?"

"She. It's a girl. She has black hair. She was wide awake."

"I went up to see Papa."

"Did you hear that Joslyn's family is leaving the train?"

"I know. I just don't know why everyone is in such a hurry. We were in a hurry to leave everything. Now we're in a hurry to get to nothing. Isn't that kind of strange?"

"It's like a game, I think. They want to get out there before other people. They're afraid all the good land or gold will be gone."

"Kind of like the line at the church supper," Retta remarked. "Some always crowd up to the front, afraid that something good might be gone before they get their turn."

"What're we goin' to do about Joslyn? We can't just let her go," Christen asked.

"We don't have any choice. But I told her we would do something special before she left."

Christen clapped her hands. "Oh, yes! But what?"

Retta leaned a little closer and whispered, "Joslyn wants to go see Two Bears and his family."

"Today?"

"Yes. Do you want to go?"

"But it's so muddy. We aren't supposed to leave camp."

"Andrew chased a gelding on the rim of the river this morning. He said it isn't too bad over there," Retta reported.

"But—but . . . will they let us?"

"I think we should at least try—for Joslyn's sake."

"I'll go with you. Who else is going?"

"I'll ask Gilson. You tell Ben. He wanted to go."

"Where will we meet?"

"At my wagon . . . in about half an hour."

"Do I need to bring a gun?" Christen asked.

"No! Of course not. The Lord will take care of us."

Ben Weaver strolled up to the wagon with his sister Christen. Joslyn waited with Retta.

"Is Gilson coming?" Christen asked.

"She doesn't feel too well," Retta replied.

Joslyn ran her fingers through her black hair. "I wonder how far west we have to go before she begins to feel better."

"Did your dad give you permission?" Ben asked.

"Papa was too busy. Mother is taking a nap, but I left her a note. How about your daddy?" she asked.

"We just said we were goin' to visit Retta," Ben admitted.

Retta glanced at her dark-haired friend. "Joslyn?"

"They didn't ask me if I wanted to pull out and leave my friends; so I didn't think I needed to ask them about this."

"If they see us head to the river, someone might holler us back," Christen warned.

"We have to take a chance."

"What are we waitin' for?" Joslyn pressed. "A sign from the Lord?"

There were shouts of "gee" and "haw" from the front of the wagon train. William galloped down the line. Mud flew up from his horse's hoofs.

Retta ran up to him. "What happened up there?"

"The California-bound are goin' to pull out at daybreak, and so we're movin' all those wagons to the front before dark."

"What can we do to help?" Retta asked.

"Our wagon isn't movin'; so just stay out of everyone's way. It will be a real mess in this mud." He rode on down the line, shouting the news at each wagon.

The others came up to Retta. "What was that all about?"

"It was a sign from the Lord," Retta reported. "Come on. They want us out of the way so they can move up the California-bound wagons. We're going to get out of the way."

She hiked away from the wagon toward the river. Ben and Christen hurried to her left, Joslyn to her right.

Ben pointed to her hand. "What's the book for?"

"I promised I'd bring Two Bears a book."

"What's he goin' to do with a book?" Joslyn asked.

"Read it, and he wants to teach his children to read."

"How about the bonnet?" Christen queried.

"It goes with the pansy-plum dress. I'm going to give it to Shy Bear. There's no reason to have one without the other. I've never worn it, you know."

"Do you really think we'll find them?" Ben asked.

"Sure. You just watch me." Retta continued to strut across the prairie.

"It's really muddy!" Christen complained.

Joslyn stomped her shoes. "I wonder what Indians do in the mud?"

"Get muddy, just like us, I suppose. Mud doesn't play favorites," Retta replied.

"And you said your Indians speak English?" Christen asked.

"They aren't my Indians, and I think only Two Bears speaks good English. He's the only one I really talked to."

Ben glanced over his shoulder. "No one is hollerin' at us to come back."

"Which means, no one knows where we've gone. We could get captured by Indians and hauled off as slaves, and no one would know about it," Christen muttered.

"Mama would know. I left her a note," Retta assured her.

"You don't have to come. Go on back," Ben told his sister.

"Oh, no. I won't miss an adventure with Retta Barre."

After several minutes they reached the brush by the side of the river. The sandy soil was still wet, but it was not as sticky as the clay soil of the wagon trail. Retta led them to the southeast along the river.

"Are you sure this is the way?" Ben asked.

"Of course I'm sure," Retta replied.

"If it's so easy to find, how come the colonel and Mr. Bouchet couldn't find it yesterday?" Joslyn asked.

"Because Two Bears didn't want them to," Retta explained.

Ben quit hiking, took off his hat, and scratched his head. "What does Two Bears look like?"

Retta stopped and turned around. "He has buckskin pants, a cotton shirt, boots, and a red bandanna around his forehead."

"Does he have black lines painted on his cheeks and a scar on his right arm?" Ben quizzed.

Retta studied Ben's wide eyes. "No, he doesn't. Why did you ask that?"

He pointed to a man standing in the shadows of the rimrock. "Then I guess that isn't him."

Nine

That's not Two Bears!" Retta gulped.

Christen let out a yelp and pranced from one foot to the other. "He's coming this way. I think I'm going to wet my pants!"

Joslyn tugged on Retta's arm. "We'd better get back to the wagons."

Ben backed away from the girls. "I should have brought my gun."

"Say something to him, Retta," Joslyn whispered.

Christen choked, "I think I'm going to vomit. Really vomit."

Ben continued to back away. "Do something, Retta!"

She held her breath and puffed out her cheeks.

"If we ran in four different directions, he could only chase one of us," Ben blurted out.

"No," Christen wailed. "It would be me. I'm scared. I want to go back right now!"

As the tall man with buckskin trousers and bare chest approached, the others crouched behind Retta.

"Do something," Ben prodded again.

Retta clutched her arms against her chest, sucked in a big breath, and blurted out, "My name is Retta Barre, and I'm a friend of Two Bears; so you'd better behave yourself."

The man stopped. Other than the big knife sheathed to his trousers, she could not see any weapon. He shouted at them. There was an urgency but no emotion in his voice.

"What did he say, Retta?" Joslyn asked.

"How should I know?"

Ben pulled the brim of his hat over his ears. "I don't think he's very happy."

"I really am going to vomit," Christen sobbed.

Retta pointed to her chest and waved her arms in the direction of the wagon train. "My friends and family are right over that hill, and they have lots of guns!" She held her hands up as if cradling a rifle.

The man stopped about ten feet in front of them and stared across the bluff of the river.

"Good work, Retta. You just told him where there are guns to steal," Ben murmured.

"I don't think he understood anything," Joslyn said.

Retta rubbed her nose and curled her lip. "What was I supposed to say?"

"I'm going to die a horrible death," Christen moaned. "I just know I am."

"I think we should run now!" Ben insisted.

"No!" Christen screamed. "I'm too scared to run! Please, please, please, don't leave me!"

"Maybe I should go get help," Ben suggested as he backed away from the girls.

The Indian reached down and jerked out his buckhorn-handled hunting knife.

"Then again, maybe I shouldn't." Ben pulled off his felt hat and chewed on the brim.

"We have to do something," Joslyn said and shoved Retta forward.

"I'm Red Bear!" she announced.

"What difference does that make?" Ben scoffed.

The man paused and pointed to his own chest. "Popa he nau ana nan wan."

"Is that his name?" Joslyn asked.

Retta puffed out her cheeks and bit her lip. "Popa?"

The man nodded.

"Popa . . . you see I have this friend named Two Bears, and he's a Shoshone."

"Shoshone?" the man repeated.

"Yes, and . . ."

The man spat in the dirt and growled, "Shoshone!"

"I don't think he likes the Shoshone," Joslyn said.

Retta pointed at the man. "Are you Shoshone?"

An angry shout followed. "He nau ana nan wan!"

"Nice work, Retta," Joslyn gasped. "Now he's really mad at us."

Christen dropped to her knees. "Lord, if You are coming back to this earth, please do it right now! Come, Lord Jesus!"

The man grabbed Retta's arm.

Christen wailed.

"Don't you grab hold of me!" Retta demanded as she pulled her arm back. "You're just a bully. You think because I'm a girl I won't fight you?"

Joslyn grabbed Retta's other arm. "What are you doing?" she cried out.

Ben bolted toward the river.

Retta yanked her arm away from Joslyn, and when she did, her fist slammed into the startled Indian, and he dropped his knife. He scooped it up with a scream and grabbed Retta by the hair.

She puffed out her cheeks. *So this is what it's like right before you die? Oh, poor Mama!*

The Indian froze when someone shouted from brush to the southwest.

"Oh no!" Christen cried. "More Indians."

"That's Two Bears!" Retta shouted. "Two Bears, tell Popa to let me go!"

Two Bears sat on a small wool blanket on the back of a buckskin horse. He pointed a musket at the Indian and shouted something. Other riders shouted back in the brush behind Two Bears.

Popa studied the horizon, released Retta's hair, and shoved his knife back into the sheath. He turned around and jogged back into the brush along the river.

Joslyn shouted and clapped her hands. "He left!"

Ben meandered back to the girls. "I reckon I don't need to go for help now."

Christen struggled to her feet. "Thank You, Jesus. Thank You, Jesus. I meant it—I'll be a missionary in India and never get married and wear those ugly dresses and everything."

"What did you say?" Joslyn asked her.

"Eh . . . nothing," Christen gulped. She wiped her eyes on her dress sleeves.

Two Bears trotted toward Retta, and behind him came his two older sons and then several other members of his family.

"There's one wearing your purple dress!" Joslyn called out.

"That's Shy Bear," Retta reported. "It's pansy plum."

"We should go back to the wagons," Ben urged.

"But these are my friends," Retta protested. "These are the ones we came to see."

"I say we should get back," Ben asserted. "I've seen enough Indians."

"I'm not leaving without Retta," Christen said.

"I'm not leaving until I talk to Two Bears," Retta insisted.

Ben jammed his hat back on. "I guess I should stay then."

"You're afraid to go anywhere without Retta, too," Christen murmured.

Retta put the pansy-plum gingham bonnet on her head and then took it off and held it out toward the young girl on the gray horse. "This is for you, Shy Bear."

The young girl slid down off the horse, sprinted up to Retta, took the bonnet with a giggle, and ran back to her waiting horse.

Two Bears rode up to Retta and then signaled for the two young men to follow the Indian into the brush along the river.

"Who was that Indian, Two Bears? He scared us. Was he a friend of yours? I don't think he was Shoshone. I thought for sure he was going to scalp me. I didn't mean to punch him that hard. My hand slipped. What are you doing down here? Where is Lucy Two Bears and your baby? I'm surely glad you came along."

Two Bears slipped off his pony and squatted on his haunches next to Retta. She squatted down beside him.

"My wife and baby are back at camp. We came to see if Red Bear needed any help, of course."

"Well, I needed help. I think he really was going to kill us."

Two Bears glanced over at her companions.

"Oh!" Retta exclaimed. "This is my friend Joslyn, and this is Christen."

"Retta and me have been best friends ever since we were three!" Christen called out.

"And this is Ben," Retta announced.

"Benweaver!" Two Bears grinned.

Ben jammed his hands into his corduroy trousers. "How did he know my name?"

Two Bears turned to Retta. "He is your boyfriend?"

"No," Ben blurted out.

A scowl replaced Two Bear's smile.

"But we are very good friends," Ben added.

Retta and Two Bears were still squatting, the others standing, when the two young men rode back and said something to Two Bears.

"Who was that Indian?" Retta asked.

"His name is Tall Owl."

"He didn't treat us very nice."

Two Bears drew a feather in the mud. "He's Arapaho."

"What does that mean?"

"It means my family and I are in very big danger," Two Bears explained. "This is Arapaho country."

"Don't the Shoshone get along with the Arapaho?" she asked.

"No."

"Where is he going?"

"Back to his camp, I suppose."

"How far away is that?"

"I hope it is far. He will gather his warriors and come after my family."

"Will they come after the wagon train?"

"I don't think so, but they may try to steal your horses."

"What will you do?" Retta asked.

"Try to avoid being killed. I want to take my family to Fort Bridger. But we have to stay away from the Arapaho and the Cheyenne and, of course, the Sioux. I had hoped to follow your wagon train for a while, but now that the Arapaho know, it might be more difficult."

"You speak very good English," Ben blurted out from his place behind the girls.

"So do you," Two Bears replied.

"Why do you want to go to Fort Bridger?" Retta quizzed.

"Because I like it better than living with the Cherokee down in the Territory."

Retta glanced down. "Oh, I almost forgot! Here is a book. It was the only one I could find extra right now." She handed him the small book.

Two Bears's eyes lit up. "I have never had a book of my own before. It will be a treasure." He looked at the cover. "*Pil-grim Pro-guess?*"

"Yes, it's called *Pilgrim's Progress,* and it's one of my favorite books," Retta said.

His grin filled his brown face and made his mouth seem unusually large. "And now it is my favorite book."

"I thought it was your only book," Joslyn commented.

"Yes, isn't that a coincidence?" He turned to Retta. "What is it about?"

"A man on a great journey to heaven to see God, who sometimes gets sidetracked and has many adventures along the way."

"That is good. I shall learn it all. I would like to take that journey to heaven myself someday."

Two Bears stood and waved to one of the boys on horseback. His son trotted over to them and handed him a leather bundle.

"These are for you," Two Bears proclaimed.

"My moccasins!" Retta squealed.

"You got beaded knee-high moccasins for one old book?" Joslyn marveled.

"I've got a book," Ben declared.

Two Bears peered around the girls at Ben Weaver. "Is it Red Bear's favorite book?"

"Eh, no, probably not. It's a penny-press novel about a pirate."

Two Bears thumbed through the book as if looking at illustrations. "Are you going to stay to eat supper with us, Red Bear? Your friends are welcome also."

Retta looked at the others. "No, we should get back. We have to help at the wagon train. The California wagons are going to break away and go ahead of the rest of us."

"I have been to California," he informed her.

"California is a long ways away," Ben said skeptically.

"Yes, I went there with Joseph Walker."

Ben's mouth dropped open. "Really?"

Two Bears sketched a bird in the mud. "I went to Washington, D.C., with Kit Carson and spoke with President Polk once."

"You met the president of the United States!" Ben gasped.

"He gave me a medal on a blue ribbon. I traded it for a pony."

"I like your Indian, Retta," Joslyn said.

"Red Bear is part of our family. Look at her dark skin and broad nose." He grinned. "I thought she was part Indian. When I saw her slug the Arapaho, I *knew* she was Shoshone. He will not forget Red Bear."

Ben cleared his throat and inched a little closer. "Can we have Indian names, too?"

Two Bears rubbed his hairless chin. "You may have any name you choose."

"But we would like you to give us real Indian names," Christen urged.

"Oh, I get to be the naming chief, do I?"

"Yes, please," Joslyn said.

"Would you like the Indian version or the English?"

"The English," Joslyn replied. She squatted down next to Retta.

"What is your name?" he asked.

"Joslyn Jouppi."

"Youpy?"

She locked her fingers and draped her hands over the top of her head. "Sort of like that."

"It sounds like a Comanche word for 'river.' And you have black hair. You were brave to stand by Red Bear's side. So perhaps you should be 'River Raven.'"

Joslyn clapped her hands. "Oh, yes! I love it!"

"How about me?" Ben said.

"I watched you with the Arapaho, Benweaver."

"Yes?"

"I think I should call you 'The-Boy-Who-Runs-Away.'"

Ben jammed his hands in his pockets. "I—I was goin' for help," he stammered. "I was jeopardizing my life in order to go for help for the girls."

Two Bears raised his eyebrows. "Then you may name yourself."

"How about Ben's sister Christen?" Retta asked.

"Perhaps she could be 'Weeping Willow.' She shed many tears."

"I like the Willow part," Christen said. "But I don't always cry. At least I didn't vomit."

"Your name is Weaver also?" Two Bears asked.

"Yes."

"Then you shall be 'Willow Weaver.'"

Christen clutched Retta's hand. "I like it. Do you like it?"

Retta nodded.

"I think this whole name thing is dumb," Ben grumbled.

"It was your idea," Christen reminded him.

"It's still dumb," he mumbled.

Retta stood and walked with Two Bears back to his horse. "When will I get to see you?"

"Perhaps I will come and visit you again."

"Again?" Joslyn choked.

"I always visit my family," he answered. "Perhaps Red Bear is my little sister. I will have to ask my mother about that."

"You . . . have a mother?" Christen blurted out. "I mean, everyone has a mother, but . . . never mind."

Two Bears put his arm on Retta's shoulder. "Now, Red Bear, go back to the wagons. Don't let them come out looking for me. I need to move my family where the Arapaho won't find us."

Retta and the others watched until Two Bears and his family disappeared into the brush along the river. Ben led the way back toward the wagons. The three girls trailed along.

"I think this has been the most exciting day of my life," Joslyn said. "It is so strange. The day started out boring. Then it got so terribly sad. And now it turned out wonderful."

"I really thought we were going to die or worse," Christen declared.

"What could be worse than dying?" Joslyn asked, then corrected herself. "Oh! Yes . . . don't answer that. I just knew that he was going to scalp Retta. Did you see the look in his eyes? I can't believe we lived through that!"

"I can't believe she slugged him in the stomach," Ben added.

"It was sort of an accident. I was mad."

"And then to have Retta's Indian come and save us . . . well, I didn't know whether to laugh or cry. I know one thing—I'm never going to wander off beyond sight of the wagons again," Christen asserted.

"Unless you're with Retta," Joslyn said.

"I wasn't all that much help," Retta replied.

"Are you kidding? You stood in front of all of us, between us and that savage. You punched him and challenged him."

"But I couldn't have stopped him."

"Well, I felt a whole lot better having you there," Joslyn insisted.

"You know how you have a bad dream and wake up scared," Christen said. "And then you pull a blanket over your head and feel better? Well, you were our blanket, Retta."

Retta reached out and held hands with both Christen and Joslyn.

Lord, this is what was missing. I needed to be something besides a little girl who carries buffalo chips. My friends needed me, and I was there. If nothing else exciting happens on this trip, that will last a lifetime. They didn't need Lerryn. They didn't need William. They didn't need Andrew. They needed Retta Barre!

Today, Lord, I like being me.

Ben Weaver let out a long sigh. "Eh, Retta . . . Christen and Joslyn are right. You were the rock we hid behind. I reckon I didn't know I would be that scared."

Retta grinned from ear to ear. *Lord, I really, really like being me!*

"Here," Joslyn offered, "do you want Retta to hold your hand, too?"

Ben and Retta both pulled back in unison. "No!"

Christen and Joslyn giggled.

They reached the crest of the knoll and spotted the activity at the wagons. Ben turned to the girls. "I don't want any of you to ever tell anyone the name that Indian gave me," he warned.

"But you did run," Christen observed.

"And you are very swift," Joslyn added.

"Like an antelope that runs from danger," Retta mused. "Perhaps your name should be 'Swift Antelope.'"

Ben's eyes lit up. He threw his shoulders back. "Now that is a good name."

Retta put her hand on his shoulder as if to knight him. "Then your Indian name shall be 'Swift Antelope.'"

Ben flashed his dimpled smile. "Honest?"

"Yes. If anyone comes up to us and asks what Benweaver's Indian name is, I shall say, 'Swift Antelope.'"

"You're a real pal." He reached up and put his hand on top of hers.

Joslyn and Christen giggled.

Retta grinned. "That's me—Retta, the pal."

Ben dropped his hand to his side. "I think I'll go tell Ansley my Indian name."

Retta held her breath and puffed out her cheeks as he sprinted across the muddy prairie.

Joslyn tugged Retta's arm, and the three girls continued their trek. "Come on, Red Bear, ol' pal. I still say he should be called 'The-Boy-Who-Runs-Away.'"

For a list of other books
by this author
write:
Stephen Bly
Winchester, Idaho 83555
or check out his website:
www.blybooks.com